Snow White:

A Survival Story

Snow White:

A Survival Story

Anna J.

www.urbanbooks.net

Urban Books, LLC
97 N18th Street
Wyandanch, NY 11798

ISBN 13: 978-1-60162-561-8
ISBN 10: 1-60162-561-8

First Mass Market Paperback Printing September 2013
First Trade Paperback Printing October 2009
Printed in the United States of America

10 9 8 7 6 5 4 3 2 1

This is a work of fiction. Any references or similarities to actual events, real people, living or dead, or to real locales are intended to give the novel a sense of reality. Any similarity in other names, characters, places, and incidents is entirely coincidental.

Distributed by Kensington Publishing Corp.
Submit Wholesale Orders to:
Kensington Publishing Corp.
C/O Penguin Group (USA) Inc.
Attention: Order Processing
405 Murray Hill Parkway
East Rutherford, NJ 07073-2316
Phone: 1-800-526-0275
Fax: 1-800-227-9604

Part One

The pain was preparation for my destiny . . .
—Kirk Franklin

Prologue

Ode to the Streets

You can't hide from the streets. As soon as you open your door and step outside, the streets is right there waiting for you. The streets almost lurk, though . . . undetected. Just kind of pacing back and forth outside your door, waiting for the perfect time to attack. Following behind you for blocks, waiting for you to sleep on 'em. See, the streets are conniving, leading you to believe that they got your back, but on the real, you out here on your own. Survival of the fittest, only the strong survive, and all that bullshit. Hell, the streets are there even when you ain't.

Oh, and don't think for a second that since you done moved up out the hood it's long gone, because the hood has a habit of following you. No matter how far you move away, the hood is only two blocks down and one block over. Or are you one of those silly bitches that try to escape the hood, but mistakenly bring it with you? The streets will mold you, though. Will take you and shape you into what it wants you to be, until you can get it in your head what you need to be if you ever decide to become a free thinker.

So I pose this question to you: Will you follow, or will you lead? Ultimately, the choice is yours, but you better make a decision quick because the streets are impatient, and at the very moment you hesitate . . . it's lights out.

Journey Clayton

January 2, 1998

"Now, Journey, remember how I told you to do it, baby," my mother, Carla, said to me in a barely audible voice as I shuffled around the room, gathering up the supplies I needed to help my mom get better.

"I remember, Momma. I had to get a cotton ball from the bathroom."

For the past year or so, I'd been performing an unthinkable task for my mother that I was way too ashamed to tell anyone about. At nine years old, I should have been playing with my dolls, or outside skipping rope and playing hopscotch with my friends. For me, those days were long gone, as I was given the task of taking care of my mother while the deadly virus known to the world as AIDS ate what was left of the shell she called a body.

Carefully setting the syringe, a bottle cap from a discarded Miller Lite bottle I'd found in the hallway, a vial of crack known on the streets as Snow White, and a small cup of water on the table, I swiftly went through the task of cooking up the illegal drug before expertly drawing it up into the syringe and tapping the side of it to get out the excess air. My mother's eyes had that glazed look they always had before she was about to get a hit, and a long thread of saliva dangled and swung from her chin in the breeze the fan was blowing from the window. Never mind the fact that it was the dead of winter; she had hot flashes that she couldn't control, and needed cool air on her at all times.

My mother was sick, and in my mind, the medicine that she took for her virus wasn't enough to put her to sleep. Moving the cover back from off of her dried and cracked feet, I desperately searched for a vein so that I could give my mother the relief she needed. The veins in her legs had long been gone, and were covered with ash that was so white it looked as if she had been rolling around in flour. The veins I had been using on the side of her neck were useless, leaving her feet as the only option.

Taking the belt that was hanging from the closet door, I looped it around my mother's ankle and tightened it to cut off the blood supply, causing the one good vein she had left between her

toes to bulge. With tears stinging my eyes, I stead-
ied my shaking hands as best I could and took the
filled syringe from the table, careful not to drop it
like I did the last time. After all, I was only nine
years old, and bound to make a mistake.

Pricking my mother's skin with the almost-
dull point, I first pulled the syringe out like I'd
done so many times before. I needed to see the
blood bubble up at the tip to make sure I had
indeed hit the vein, not missing it like I had the
previous day. Slowly I began to inject the poison
into my mother's system, and at the same speed,
the top of my mother's body began to slump in
a slow nod, letting me know I had done my job.

Once the syringe was empty, I took it into the
bathroom that was connected to the room and
flushed it with bleach and water to try to keep
it clean, knowing that it was already too late.
The bug you caught from sharing needles done
already got to my mother. After putting up the
utensils I used to give my mother her much-
needed fix, I tucked her into the bed carefully
and kissed her on the forehead. I turned the television to Fox 29 so that if she woke up, she could
watch her favorite shows.

Now, on the other side of the door sat a de-
mon that lurked around my household. At nine

years old, my mother was the least of my problems. I approached the neatly kept living room
in a juice-stained wife beater that was so tight
it made me look like a little boy. Only my long,
sandy-brown ponytail and plastic pink moon-
shaped earrings gave any indication that I was
actually born a girl. I sighed deeply at the task
before me.

Turning the corner, I paused before approaching Vince, the neighborhood drug dealer who
made it all possible for my mother to keep getting her fix. Standing in front of him in a pair
of dingy My Little Pony printed underwear that
said Tuesday on the back when it was clearly
Thursday was embarrassing for me, but I had to
do what I had to do. My mom needed her medicine.

Stepping out of my panties, I climbed up on
the couch next to twenty-three-year-old Vince
and loosened his pants, ready to perform. After
all, it was for my mother, and my mother was all
I had.

"Now, remember how I told you to do it,
baby," Vince said in a deep, husky voice that
scared the shit out of me. I tried to act like it
didn't bother me at all.

Honestly, I couldn't believe my own uncle
would do such horrible things to me. I just didn't

understand it. You were supposed to be loved by your family, not made to do things that I was sure were reserved only for adults. I couldn't cry, though. Tears didn't mean a thing to Vince, and would only prolong the situation. He was supposed to love me, but I felt hurt and confused, and he never attempted to provide answers, just demanded that he stay in control. I was too afraid for my life to do anything but stay in line, but I hated Vince with everything in me.

Vince had a thing for young girls, and seeing me in the state that I was in gave him the advantage. He convinced me that I didn't want to be put into foster care, so the only way I could be with my mother was to make sure she stayed alive. If doing this to get her supply was the only option, then that was my only option.

Vince broke down all the rules to me from the very beginning: I did what he told me to do, and he'd keep supplying that Snow White for my mother. All I wanted was for my mom to get better, and I was too young to realize I was making a deal with the devil, so that's just the way it worked out. But little girls grow up fast in the hood.

It wouldn't be until much later that I learned how to flip what I learned to get what I wanted, but for Vince, that wouldn't be a good thing.

After all, he did promise his brother Jimmy, my father, that he'd take care of the family as he lay in a hospital bed breathing his last breaths after a stabbing that punctured his lungs and heart.

In Vince's eyes, he didn't feel he was doing anything wrong. He was merely preparing me for the real world; in his mind, if it wasn't him, it would be some other young cat around the way. Shit, he was helping me out by keeping it in the family, or so he thought. In reality, he had my young mind twisted. If family would do you like this, what anyone else was bound to do didn't hold any weight.

Not even bothering to look at me after he zipped up his pants, he threw three vials on the table like he was shooting dice. I scrambled for the drugs like I was the one that had the addiction and not my mother. Three was only enough for about a day and a half because I usually gave my mother a shot in the morning and at night, so I mentally prepared myself to see Vince in about two days.

Running my bath water once he was gone, I rinsed away the day with a few pieces of balled-up soap that had melted down from previous use. I hoped my situation would get better soon.

Once I got into my room, I hung the pair of panties on the windowsill next to the only other two I owned, which were already there. I had hand washed them in the sink earlier. I only owned four pairs: Tuesday, Friday, and Sunday. What happened to the other days-of-the-week panties that I used to have are beyond me, but I worked with what I had and kept it moving. I hoped they would be dry by the morning, or else I would have to wear an old pair of shorts under my jeans.

I moisturized my skin with lotion from the Dollar Tree, even though I knew I would still be ashy in the morning, afterwards smoothing out my paper-thin Care Bear comforter over my body. Taking my stuffed rabbit, Hippity Hop, into my arms, I cuddled up and fell asleep, hoping that the nightmares that normally haunted me would let me rest on this night. I knew the mustard sandwich I ate for dinner wasn't enough, and I closed my eyes tight so that the growling from my stomach wouldn't play too loudly in my ears. Thinking about the way my life was going saddened me, but it was for my mother, and I'd go to the end of the earth for her. Besides all that, she was all I had, and I needed her around.

Joey Street

Wrong Place at the Wrong Time

Friday, 3:00 a.m.

"Man, I know you ain't getting scared now. All we gotta do is walk in there and take the money. It's only two of 'em in there, so it'll be a piece of cake," Bunz said to me as we blazed an L in the parked car across the street from the African hair braiding shop on the corner of Fortieth and Lancaster Avenue.

It was three o'clock in the damn morning, and I knew my girl Shanyce was gonna be mad as shit when I got home, but I had to get this paper. We had been scouting this place for like two weeks now, and figured that Marie's African Hair Braiding Shop was getting mad paper.

I saw the heavyset sista with the cute face walk into the shop around seven-thirty that night, and I thought for sure they were going to turn her away. I was trying to find any excuse not to go through with the robbery because every time I dealt with Bunz, it always ended up in a tragedy. When I saw a woman who must have been the owner get on the horn and make a few calls, and a half hour later a younger looking African girl pull up to the door, I knew they would be in there for the rest of the night.

"Nah, I ain't scared, nigga. Just don't go in there getting all trigger happy and shit like you did the last time. No one has to die."

Bunz turned and looked at me like he couldn't believe what I was saying, but I knew he got off on fear and sometimes didn't make the best decisions. In a hostage situation, your adrenaline is pumping, and the weed that we'd been smoking on all day made him think irrationally at the most inopportune times. That's why the last time we did a stickup I found myself spreading peanut butter all over a dead woman's body while he yanked her teeth out of her mouth so that the rats and vermin would eat her and no one would be able to identify her body. Three days later they found the girl. I tried like hell to keep a straight face as I watched the story breaking on the ten o'clock news, but it was killing me on the inside.

Lancaster Avenue was popping like it was three in the afternoon instead of the a.m. hours that we were presently in, so we waited until it died down some to make our move. Sporting all black, with a Yankees fitted pulled down over my eyes, we walked across the street like it wasn't nothing. The young girl and the client never saw us coming. We stood on the side of the door out of view of them, just to see who would walk up. I could see inside the shop from my viewpoint, and although the braider and the client were holding a conversation, they both looked exhausted and ready to go home.

We were about to make our move when a bunch of loud, drunk-ass girls turned the corner where the news stand was located, after getting off the 40 bus. We didn't need any witnesses, so we waited for them to get almost to the Murry's food store next to the barbershop up the block before we did what we had to do.

"You ready, Street?" Bunz said to me under his breath, calling me by my last name. I wanted to say that I wasn't ready, but I was already there, so I had to make it do what it was gonna do. I could see the excitement of a possible kill in his eyes, but I was hoping he'd chill out tonight. Nightmares from so many dead bodies were already haunting my dreams, and I couldn't take it anymore.

"As ready as I'll ever be," I mumbled back, feeling the handle on the sawed-off shotgun I held in the small of my back.

From what we observed over the last couple of weeks, there was a resident that lived on top of the braid shop that kept traffic coming in and out, so we just acted like we were waiting for him to come down and let us in as we stood in the cramped hallway outside of the shop. We closed the gate behind us so that no one could just rush in.

Both the client and the stylist looked up at us, but quickly turned back to their conversation. I noticed that the woman who was getting her hair done was cute to be a big girl, and under any other circumstances, I probably would have tried to get at her. Tonight, I was on a mission, but if I ever saw her again after this day, it was on.

The client must have said something to the girl because she had a scared look on her face, and the girl that was braiding her hair stopped what she was doing and moved toward the door to lock it. I was wondering why in hell the door wasn't locked in the first damn place, but she didn't even get a chance to touch it. Bunz kicked open the door and pulled his gun, causing the girl to stumble back to her chair.

My eyes were quick, and I saw the woman that was getting her hair braided dial some numbers on her phone and turn the volume down before placing her phone under the shelf. I knew for sure she had called the cops. Instead of alerting Bunz to the situation, I tried my best to speed it up because I knew the law was on its way. If he knew that, he would kill them. As he always said, "The dead can't testify in court."

"Give me all your fuckin' money," Bunz shouted at the two women, who were now shedding tears. I felt like shit at that moment, but I needed this paper.

"There's no money here. They took it away earlier," the African said in a heavy accent, and I knew what she was saying to be true. There was another African woman in the shop with her earlier who could have easily been her mother, and knowing the area that we were in, she more than likely took the money when she left. I guess since we had staked the place for so long, Bunz wanted to get whatever he could get, whether it was from the owners or the customers. I was in it to win it, so no matter how ridiculous I thought the plan was, I had to go through with it.

"Let's just go, man. Ain't nothing poppin' in here," I said to Bunz, trying to quickly diffuse the situation because I knew the law was on its way. I couldn't do time. It just wasn't in the cards.

"Man, fuck that," Bunz said with that wild look in his eyes he got every time a bad situation was about to turn worse. A part of me just wanted to jet on his ass, but he was my boy, and besides all that, he had the car keys.

"Yo, I saw the other shorty leave earlier. She more than likely took the money with her."

"Yo, nigga, shut up. I know it's some money in this muthafucka, and that big bitch needs to empty her bag too. I know she got some rent money up in there."

I couldn't even look at her. Instead, I looked out the window for any telltale signs that the jakes were heading our way; but everything was quiet. Looking back at Bunz, I could see him starting to get antsy, and his eyes had glazed over. Vince had warned me about fucking with him, but my dumb ass didn't listen.

Just as I was turning my attention back to the situation at hand, I witnessed the brains of the young African girl fly from her head in slow motion and splatter a bloody mess in the mirror. The client fainted on sight, but Bunz took it to her anyway. He put the silencer so close to her head that the spark bounced off her earrings, and at that very moment, my stomach began to turn.

He rifled through her pocketbook and came up with about fifteen hundred dollars inside of a Bank of America deposit envelope. Either she just cashed her check, or she was going to deposit it. Too bad neither would ever go down.

Bunz looked around the shop, but he found no cash. Cursing up a storm, he made his way to the front of the shop, only to notice the open cell phone sitting under the counter. Going over to it, he picked it up to see 911 displayed across the call screen. I just shook my head. It was one of those kinds of situations where you ain't had no business doing what you were doing, but you did it anyway, and now look at you.

"Come on, nigga. Let's roll," he said after he turned the phone off and tucked it in his pocket.

When we got back to the car in front of the Lincoln Fried Chicken spot, he roofed the phone just in case it had a GPS hookup in it, and we got in the car and jetted. Shanyce was gonna definitely be mad because the break down from that fifteen was only seven-fifty a piece, and she needed our son Khalid's tuition money ASAP.

"Just drop me off on the corner, nigga," I said to Bunz as we approached my block. I had to face the music, but on the real, I wasn't ready.

Journey Clayton

Back in the Swing of Things

I had to give my mom her shot before I went to school.

The one thing my uncle did right was send me to private school. I guess he didn't want anyone around the way asking me questions about my mom's situation, or about him, for that matter.

It was just after the New Year, and I went into 1998 optimistic that my life would change in a major way this year. The thing is, life is always changing, and it's how you deal with it that makes the difference.

I battled with the high winds and snowfall as I walked the five or six blocks to school from Fifty-fourth and Greenway to Fifty-fifth and Chester Avenue to the Evelyn Graves Christian Academy, located on the corner across the street from the Salt & Pepper Deli. It didn't seem to matter what time of day it was, rain or shine; the deli was always packed with drunks and drug addicts, who copped from the drug dealers that huddled in the back of the store so that the cops wouldn't see them conducting business. It was like a one stop shop, where you could get your drink, your high, and your munchies all in the same place at the same time.

I hated the looks that those old men gave me because it was the same look Vince gave me when he came by. I couldn't wrap my mind around what these grown-ass men saw in my underdeveloped body, but instead of inquiring, I picked up the pace to get past them so that I could get to school on time.

I pulled my black pea coat, which was missing two of the four buttons, tighter around my neck as another gush of wind threatened to blow me back in the direction I came from. After struggling to open the heavy door of the school building, I rushed to my cubby before anyone else could see me. I wanted to hang up my coat and sit down before anyone noticed my high-water pants and dingy socks. Vince said that if I acted right he would buy me some more school uniforms, but that had yet to happen, and I was past holding my breath waiting on it.

I was rearranging the few things I had in my desk when I looked up just in time to see Khalid and his dad exchange a loving hug before he left. I didn't know his father's name, but I saw him hanging out with Vince on more than one occasion, so I figured he was bad news, too. Khalid was so cute, though, and I'd be lying if I said I didn't have a small crush on him, even though I wasn't crazy enough to let him know it. Besides, I think he had a thing for Gina, the prettiest girl in the class.

When the teacher came in, I noticed that she seemed upset, and she looked like she may have been crying. Her eyes were bloodshot, and her face looked flushed and tearstained. I also noticed I didn't see Kareema in class yet, and I said a quick prayer in hopes that nothing was wrong with her. Kareema never missed a day of school, and was usually one of the first people in class in the morning. Not that we were friends or anything, but out of all the people in my class, she was one of the few that was actually nice to me.

The principal came into the classroom shortly after with the *Daily News* folded in half across his arm. From what I could make out from my seat, it looked like a picture of Kareema's mother displayed across the front of the paper. "Class, I have an announcement to make," Mr. Carpenter said after he excused our teacher, Mrs. Solomon, out of the class. I could feel my chest getting tighter by the second, and a part of me didn't want to hear the bad news.

Once he had our attention, he informed us that over the weekend, Kareema's mother was killed while getting her hair done at a braid shop. He gave us a packet of information to take home to our parents and told us to remain in our seats until Mrs. Solomon was able to come back to class. It was like the room was stuck on pause as each of us absorbed the news. Some of us were crying and some were just in a state of shock at what occurred. I felt horrible for Kareema because in my heart, I knew I would be losing my mother soon, too, and I wasn't ready. A tragic loss like that is devastating, and I prayed that she would be okay one day. It took Mrs. Solomon more than a half hour to come back to class, and when she did finally arrive, her eyes were bloodshot. I overheard Mrs. Martin, our music teacher and Mrs. Solomon's best friend, tell the principal that Mrs. Solomon and Kareema's mother were real close and that she was taking her death pretty hard. I didn't really understand the concept of death all like that, but I knew that I lost a lot of people that were close to me, and I could feel her pain. The way my uncle Vince explained it was that we all had to die some day, but that didn't stop it from being devastating, whether you were expecting it or not.

I could see Mrs. Solomon trying to get herself together, and I wondered why they didn't just ask her to leave.

For most of the morning, we read silently at our desks until it was time for recess. It was too cold for us to play outside, so we were escorted to the music room, where we were left to play amongst ourselves. On this day, though, no one did. We kind of just sat around, tinkering with the instruments and talking amongst ourselves. I was in the corner by myself, making a card for Kareema out of construction paper, so that I would have something to give her when she got back. She lost her mother, and I knew that was hard for her, and I wanted her to know that she could talk to me if she wanted to.

I wasn't paying much attention to anyone else in the class, and was a little startled when I looked up and saw Khalid standing in front of me. I instantly blushed, not believing that he had actually noticed me. I looked at him quickly then put my head back down, too shy to make eye contact. What did I do to deserve this attention? As bad as I wanted to know, I would never ask; but he didn't take long in satisfying my curiosity.

"Whatchu doin'?" Khalid asked, taking a seat on the floor next to me. My face felt flushed, and the room spun briefly before I was able to focus and answer his question.

"Making a card for Kareema," I responded in a barely audible voice as I continued to cut out heart shapes on the construction paper. I could barely breathe with him being this close to me, and I hoped he couldn't feel how nervous I was.

"That's cool."

"Yeah."

"So, umm . . . if you want, maybe we can study after school sometimes. Either at your house or mine. You live on Grays Avenue, right?"

"Yeah."

"Cool," he said to me with a slight smile on his face.

"Whenever you want, let me know."

Before I could respond, the school principal came back to get us so that we could finish with the rest of our day. Mrs. Solomon was gone when we got back, and we were informed that she had left for the day. The rest of the afternoon was pretty gloomy, and we didn't really do much of anything besides reading and going over our spelling words in a mini spelling bee that Mrs. Solomon had scheduled on our agenda for the day. After a long, dragged-out day, we were finally able to leave.

I waited until all of the other students got their belongings from the cubbies before I went over to put on my coat, because I didn't want anyone to see how raggedy my coat was. I took my time putting my stuff in my book bag, hoping that everyone was gone.

I put my book bag on my back and made my way out to the front of the school just in time to see Khalid standing on the corner. At first I started to act like I didn't see him, but I had to go home that way, so it was senseless to do that. I got up the nerve to go over to where he was standing, waiting for the light to turn green. I was hoping he would just cross, but he didn't.

"Girl, what took you so long coming out? I thought you were going to let me freeze," he said with a smile, holding out his hand for me to hold it. I didn't reply; I simply smiled back and took his hand as we started crossing the street.

I thought he was going to let my hand go once we got to the other side, but he held it as we walked and talked all the way home. I was on cloud nine, not believing my fortune on this afternoon. The cutest boy in the class had me by the hand and was walking me home. He could have easily chosen to walk with Gina and her stuck-up friends, but he chose me. I didn't feel the wind or the snow on this day; for me, it felt like springtime with him walking next to me.

The closer we got to home, the slower I walked, because I didn't want it to end. Come to find out he lived right around the corner from me on Glenmore Avenue, about three houses from the corner.

We stood looking at each other for what felt like an eternity, until he suddenly leaned over and kissed my lips.

"We're going to be good friends, Journey," he said to me with a big smile on his face before taking his hand away from mine. "Don't forget to ask your mom if we can study together. We can start next Monday."

I was stuck on that corner for a good five minutes before the wind pushed me onto my block and into the house. I knew at that moment nothing could ruin my day, or so I thought. Like most children, I had chores, and since I pretty much kept our place clean, the only thing I had to do was to make sure my mom ate and had her fix for the night. Some days it went smoothly and she was able to keep all of her food down, and other days she could barely stomach a saltine cracker and vomited all over the place. I would soon see what kind of day I was having once I settled in and started making her some soup.

I put the package that the school gave us concerning Kareema's mother on the table for Vince to look at, since my mother couldn't do it. I knew I would have to see him later because I only had one more fix for my mother, and he knew I would need more for the next couple of days. I hurried through my homework so that I could feed my mom and be ready by the time he got here. He wanted me undressed when he walked in the door or else, and I didn't feel like dealing with the extra nonsense.

Heating the soup in the microwave because Vince didn't like me using the stove, I tasted it to make sure it wasn't too hot before placing a couple of saltine crackers on the side and balancing it on a plate. I walked into the room to find my mother watching television. I could see a slight tremor in her body and I knew that was because it was almost time for her medicine.

Propping the plate next to the alarm clock on the table, I began spoon-feeding her small amounts of the broth just to see how her stomach would act before I fed her noodles.

She acted like she was feeling well, but the moment I started feeding her noodles and crackers, she began to gag like it was coming back up. I rushed to the bathroom to grab some towels to catch the vomit because it would be too difficult to change her by myself if she messed up her clothes. The nurse that came to dispense her prescription medication only came once a day. My mother took medicine for AIDS, as well as heart medication. The nurse pretty much stayed long enough for two doses. Vince was responsible for giving her the last dose for the day, but I always ended up doing it. They didn't know about the dope I fed her twice daily, or if they did, nothing was ever said to me.

I looked at the clock to see that Vince was running late, and I hoped that he wouldn't have me sitting around for the rest of the night waiting like he sometimes did. I couldn't go to sleep until he got there, and I had school tomorrow, so I wanted to turn in kind of early. I thought about Khalid, too, and I didn't know what to make of it, so I decided to play it by ear and not read too much into it.

I was happy that my mom only spit up a little bit, and I was able to feed her the rest of her soup without incident. By now it was already dark and going on six o'clock. Vince was usually in the living room already waiting for me, but he wasn't out there yet, so something must have happened. I just hoped it wasn't something that kept him from bringing me what I needed.

I took a seat in front of the television and waited. I wanted to get this over with as soon as possible so that I could get back to thinking about Khalid.

Lying on the couch completely nude, I turned the television to UPN so that I could catch a little bit of my favorite show, *Good Times*, before Vince showed up. This show gave me hope sometimes, and I loved the theme song: *Ain't we lucky we got 'em?* Sometimes I wasn't so sure.

Vincent Clayton

Huggin' the Block

"Ay, yo, Street! You duckin' me, nigga?" I hollered down the street at my man Joey. Bunz told me that bullshit that went down in West Philly the other night, but I needed to hear it from someone with a level head. Usually this dude was out grindin' all day, but I hadn't seen him since that shit, and it made me suspicious about who I was dealing with.

I took a glance at my white gold Vacheron Constantin timepiece, seeing that I was running behind schedule. I was supposed to have been at my sister-in-law's house, and I knew my niece was waiting on me; but Journey had waited before, and she knew not to go to sleep before I got there. I needed to talk to her anyway, because I came up with a good idea that could make me even more money, and I'd be willing to cut her in on it if she acted right.

Journey had been cutting and cooking coke for her mom for well over a year, and I secretly used my sister-in-law as a test dummy for different shit that I got along the way. Surprisingly, Journey hadn't killed her yet. That's a skill that isn't taught, but inherited, and I needed to cash in on that immediately. She was good at math. All I had to do was teach her how to measure and bag the shit up and I was in there.

This nigga took his time getting down the block. I was getting impatient, but I didn't want to make a scene, especially since I needed answers. Bunz was acting all tightlipped and shit, only telling me what he wanted me to know, but something else happened at that braid shop that he wasn't saying.

Joey looked a little awkward as he got closer. He was holding a manila envelope tightly in his hand like it held the answers to living a longer life or something. I'd inquire about that after I found out what was really good.

"My nigga," I said to Joey, giving him a pound and a half embrace like brothers do. He looked like he was upset about some shit, and I was debating whether I wanted to know what it was. "Where you been hiding at, yo? I been tryin'a get at you all week."

"Dude, it's a lot going on right now."

"Yeah, Bunz told me about that bullshit-ass braid shop robbery that went down the other day. What I tell you about fuckin' with that dude, yo? He bad news, mark my words."

"Nigga, don't you think I know that?" He said with way too much emotion, and I knew some shit had gone down that shouldn't have. It didn't seem like he was going to come right out and tell me what it was, either, so I decided to come at him sideways to get the information.

"What's in the envelope, man?" I asked him, trying to come at another angle, but my man looked like he was about to fall apart. The longer we stood there, the more I knew something happened that Bunz wasn't telling.

"Yo, let's walk and talk," he said like he was all nervous and shit.

I started walking toward the deli over by the Ville so that I could get me a vanilla Dutch before I went to handle my business. It sounded like this dude was about to girl up on me, and I wasn't sure I was even ready for that shit.

During the walk, he started telling me about the bullshit that went down with him and Bunz down the bottom the other day. Apparently, these niggas done robbed the braid shop that

Bunz's simple ass had been plotting on for a few weeks now. The only thing is, the owner took the money when she left, and that spelled bad news for whoever was involved, especially if Bunz was the one holding the gun. He ended up shooting the young girl and the client, only coming up on a few hundred dollars that they split down the middle.

"So, what you so shook about, nigga? How many bodies you got on you now?" I asked him, being sarcastic.

See, Joey was from the streets, but not like the rest of us were. Most of us were pretty much immune to killing a nigga. We just made it do what it did and bounced, ditching that body until it showed up floating on the Schuylkill River near Bartram's Garden. I didn't give a fuck about a dead nigga, because that just meant his ass wouldn't be testifying in court. Joey, on the other hand, was still going through his nightmare stage; but I was determined to make him into a real soldier sooner than later.

"I ain't shook, nigga, so let's get that straight." Joey came back with an attitude that I wasn't expecting. It was about time he got some balls about him.

"So, what's the problem then?" I stopped right in front of the deli so that he could answer. I hoped this dude wasn't getting soft on me 'cause I swear I was not in the mood.

"This the problem, nigga," Joey said, showing me the contents of the envelope. It was from his son's school. Apparently the child of the woman that Bunz killed was in his son's class, and they sent the information home for the parents to look over. His son was in the same class as my niece, so I know that shit must have hit home.

I took the paper from him and quickly scanned the article. It said that the murder happened about three in the morning on the Friday before New Year's Day. The client involved was getting her hair done before starting her book tour, said her family. It seems that she was some kind of bestselling author from Philly and had written all these books and shit. The young girl that was doing her hair was only seventeen years old. Her mother and the family of the deceased client did the interview, and the woman's daughter, Kareema, attended the school. They had both of the women's pictures on the cover. I remembered seeing her around the way. I think she had some family out the Ville or something like that.

"So, what you gonna do, man?" I asked as I stepped into the deli to get what I came for. I knew his son must have been going through it,

and that meant that Journey probably was too.
Damn, guess I wasn't getting any head tonight.
Usually I made her sweat for this good product,
but I did have a heart somewhat. Tonight I'd just
give it to her, but she'd have to put in overtime
the next time around.

"Dude, I gotta get my son straight first."

"Yeah, I hear that, but I told you that nigga
Bunz is a knucklehead. Stop rolling out with that
dude, yo. What, you ain't eating right hustling on
the block?"

"Yeah, I'm good, man. Money just got a little
tight for a second, that's all."

"Street, honestly, you a good soldier, but you
ain't made for the stick-up business. Leave that
shit for them knuckleheads that ain't got nothing
better to do. I got something in the works, but
I'ma put you on later. Just give me a second to
get shit poppin'."

"Cool. Let me go handle my seed and I'll get at
you later."

"Later, my nigga."

"A'ight dude, later."

I checked one of my stash houses before I went
to see Journey to cop me a bag of that blueberry
and to make sure my shit was running properly.
I had a good amount of cash and product hidden
at the house with Journey and her mom because I
knew that the law would never look there.

When I walked into the crib, the first thing I noticed was the manila envelope sitting on the table. It was identical to the one Street showed me earlier. I knew I would have to sit down and say a few kind words to her about the situation, but on some real shit, I ain't give a damn. We all have to go some day, and that's just the way life works, but I knew I couldn't explain that shit to her like that.

She was naked, just the way I liked her to be, but I felt bad about it today for some reason. Five more years and I'd be tearing that ass up, and the thought of it made my dick hard, but I held it down. Journey looked at me with sad eyes and clicked the television off. She kneeled on the couch, waiting for me to sit down so that she could handle her business, but as bad as I wanted my dick sucked, I couldn't do it.

"Yo, go put some damn clothes on. I ain't in the mood for this shit right now," I lied through my teeth, the imprint of my dick pressed against my zipper telling another story. She looked hesitant at first, but the look I gave her told her she had better get moving before I changed my mind.

In ten seconds flat, she was standing in front of me, dressed in a dingy pair of panties with matching undershirt. For the first time, I took a

good look at her ashy little body and I wasn't so
sure that I was doing the right thing. But when I
thought about the magnificent head I'd trained
her to perform, I couldn't let nobody else get a
hold of that.

Pushing my thoughts to the back of my head,
I flipped through the folder that the school sent
home, sticking it in my coat pocket to read later.

"Listen, I'm gonna come back through here
tomorrow, so make sure you come straight home
after school. I need you to do something for me,
but now isn't the time to get into details."

"What about my mom's medicine? She needs
one for the morning, and I don't have anymore,"
she said in a small voice near the verge of tears.
Damn, I hated to see her cry, and tried to block
that shit out instantly.

"Here," I said, passing her one cap of Snow
White. "I'll be back tomorrow, so that should
hold you. Make sure you come straight home
so that I can take you to get some new uniforms
and shit. Then I got something I need you to do.
Understood?"

She nodded her head and held on to the vial of
drugs I had just given her like she was the fiend. I
stood up from the couch and looked at her again,
shaking my head and walking into the bedroom
to look at my sister-in-law. She looked a horrid

mess, the life gone from her body from years of getting high and shit. I wanted to feel bad for her, but she let my simple-ass brother turn her out, and now look at her. "Journey, bring your ass straight home from school tomorrow," I said to her on the way out, not bothering to wait for a response. I had been promising her school uniforms, and I figured if I laced her real fast with some fly shit and got her hair done and all that, she'd be more willing to cooperate with me on what I was trying to do.

On my way up the block, I saw this long-legged trick named Raynita that lived in the corner house next to Wanda's bar down near Fifty-fifth and Springfield. She must have been up here to cop, and I had just the thing for her ass. She turned around just in time to see me cross the street.

I felt almost bad for selling to her because she was a cutie. She had hips and ass like a mu'fucka, and a nice set of kissable titties, but you could see the use of drugs starting to wear away at her face. Her once full, dick-sucking lips started to twist from her habit, and it looked like she was missing a few teeth. Another one bites the dust. I took her through the alley and got me a chewy real quick, since fuckin' with Journey was out of the question. I even threw her a couple extra tops for doing a good job.

Back on the block, I pulled my North Face coat tighter around my neck and prepared to get on my grind. The drug game is never asleep, and as long as these dope heads had a taste for that Snow White, I'd be out there to give it to 'em. Another day, another dollar made.

Joey Street

Deal or No Deal

"Yo, Choice, man, Bunz is a fuckin' mental case, dude. I mean, I know we out here makin' it happen, but damn. Does he have to kill every damn body?"

I was sittin' up in my man Choice's house, watching a basketball game that he had recorded from the other day. This nigga had a fly-ass pad that his sisters kept in top shape for him on a weekly basis. He had some bad-ass sisters, too, and I was really feeling his sister Eve, but she knew my son's mom, so she wouldn't let me push up. Besides that, Choice was real protective over his sisters, so I wouldn't dare disrespect him like that. You know how them Jamaican niggas get, and he been done tried to kill my ass.

"I don't even know why you fuck with that dude, man. We soldiers. Why are you out frolicking with stick-up kids anyway? If your paper

looking shady, you need to holla at Vince. You
know he cool people."

"Yeah, I know. Shanyce fucked some shit up
for me, though, and I had to tap into my stash,
but it's getting handled now. I'm just pissed that
she's mad and she the one that fucked up," I said
to him, not bothering to go into detail.

Shanyce let her brother into our house to
watch Khalid because she wanted to get her
damn feet done, and this nigga dipped out with
one of my packs. She begged me not to let Vince
know because we both knew that Vince would
dead that nigga, but in the midst of all that, I had
to get that money back up before Vince started
asking questions. In the meantime, we still had
Khalid's tuition that needed to be paid for the
semester, amongst other things, and she wasn't
willing to come up off her entire check to foot the
bill. I wanted to choke the shit out of her, but after the first time I had to smack her up for some
dumb shit, I promised her that I would never put
my hands on her again. She was making it hard
to keep that promise.

Bunz talked me into doing this popcorn-ass
robbery that was supposed to have been sweet,
but that shit ended in a tragedy, as usual, leaving
me exhausted because now I couldn't sleep at

night. It fucked me up even more when I found out that the woman had a child in my little man's class, bringing that night right back to haunt me. What the fuck? I can't win for losing sometimes.

"So, how much you in for, nigga?" Choice asked me, taking his eyes off the game for a brief second. I hated looking this nigga in the eye because it was like he could see right through me.

"I'm set only eight G's now, but I'm almost in," I answered, minus the eight thousand I had already turned in. The pack that Shanyce let her brother walk out with was worth sixteen thousand, and she only contributed about five hundred to the sixteen that was owed.

"You say eight G's is all?" he asked, getting up from the couch and going into his bedroom.

I was tucked snuggly in his overstuffed chair that felt like I was wrapped in a damn cloud. Rumor had it that his shit was stuffed with thousands of dollars, but who really knew? Besides, no one had the balls to come test that nigga because he had papers.

"Yeah, nigga, that's all, but I'm working it out." I took a swig from the Mike's Hard Lemonade bottle that I brought up here with me and took a peek at my cell phone. Shanyce had called my phone at least twenty times since I'd been there, but I didn't feel like the bullshit. When she'd shown me the package that Khalid brought home from school, we got in an argument because she blamed me for pulling the trigger. I denied the fact that I was even there, but when she asked me where I got the money for Khalid's tuition, I nutted up. I wasn't expecting her to ask that question, and I had yet to get my story together, so she caught me off guard. Instead of arguing with her and having to lie, I walked out on her ass. She'd been calling me ever since.

"Problem solved," Choice said to me, dropping a bundle of hundred-dollar bills in my lap. I picked up the money and noticed $10,000 written in blue ink on the wrapper.

"Yo, I can't take this money, man. I'll figure it out."

"Take the money and get that cloud from over ya head. It's nothing to me."

"I'll still be in debt because now I'll owe you, and I'm already stressed."

"Yo, take the money. You don't have to pay it back; you just owe me one. Cool?"

"I guess, but I only need eight. It's ten in here," I said to him, skeptical about taking the cash. Owing him one could be worse than paying it back, and I wasn't sure if it was even worth it.

"It's a gift. Tell Shanyce to buy herself something pretty with it," he said, sitting back down and rolling up another L. I was stuck because I really needed the money.

The thing is, Vince got me on the block, and I was making good money, but I wasn't on lieutenant status like Choice and Bird. Them niggas was getting cake and baking pies like it was no tomorrow. I hustled the corners, and even though me and Vince were cool, I needed to either up my change or up my ranking so that I could get more money. I decided at that moment I would holla at Vince the next chance I got so we could talk about the situation.

Tucking the money away inside my jacket pocket, I decided that I wouldn't turn in all the money right away, because then Vince would want to know how I got it that fast or would think that I was moving product like that and I wasn't. Every time I turned in money, I would add two stacks on the top until the entire eight was in. That way, Vince wouldn't be too suspicious of what I was doing. I had my cash and my remaining packs hidden in my son's room in the wall inside of his closet, so we wouldn't have this same problem again. And I wouldn't tell Shanyce about the shit either. She would have to learn how this shit worked if she ain't want our asses strapped to the ceiling ass-naked, getting beat by ten niggas.

Me and Choice watched the rest of the game in silence as we passed a blunt back and forth. He had a vanilla blunt wrap loaded with blueberry sticky that tasted like a damn blueberry pie with a scoop of vanilla ice cream on top when you puffed it. That shit was that blaze that had you fucked up, and I copped a bag from him before I rolled out. I ain't want to be caught on the streets with that kind of money on me, so I made a bee-line from Choice's crib to mine so that I could stash my shit.

When I walked in, the house was dark, making me glance at my watch to see what time it was. I knew Shanyce was probably pissed because it was already ten o'clock and I was just now getting back home. I went into my son's room first, and he was sound asleep. I took that opportunity to stash my shit in his closet, using the light from my cell phone to see what I was doing. Everything was the same as I left it, meaning Shanyce hadn't found my stash yet.

Once I was done in the closet, I gave my boy a kiss on the cheek before pulling the covers up over his shoulders and leaving the room, closing the door behind me. I wanted to leave back out, but I went in the room to hear Shanyce's bullshit so I wouldn't have to hear it tomorrow.

I stood by the door to listen for the television, but I didn't hear anything, so I assumed she was asleep. Hell, I hoped she was; then I wouldn't have to hear her damn mouth.

When I finally opened the door, I saw Shanyce stretched out on the bed, looking good as shit in red lingerie and heels to match. Her long hair was pinned up in a sexy bun, with wisps of hair framing her face and neck. My dick got hard instantly, and I almost forgot that I was mad at her simple ass . . . almost.

I acted like I didn't even see her there, going over to the corner and sitting in the chair, taking my time removing the Timberland boots from my feet. She watched my every move as I stripped down to my boxers and folded my clothes neatly in a pile on the floor. Even though they were dirty from me wearing them all day, I didn't like filth, and kept my stuff together at all times.

I noticed she didn't have any panties on, and she was wearing that peach shimmer lip-gloss that I liked so much. Her titties sat up nicely under the lacy red material. Even after her having our son, her body was still tight. I resisted the urge to take her clit into my mouth and suck all the cum out of her body, but my dick was betraying me, and she could clearly see that she had me turned the fuck on.

I lay in the bed next to her and flipped on the television like I didn't even see her, turning to SportsCenter so I could watch the game high-lights. My dick was straining against my boxers, making me feel uncomfortable. I really wanted her to reach in there and release the beast, but I kept my damn mouth shut. If she wanted this dick, she was going to have to work for it.

It was almost like she read my mind. She didn't waste a second reaching in and grabbing a hold of my throbbing dick. I wasn't down to my knees with the shit, but the seven inches I had was heavy enough to knock the bottom out a pussy, and she loved every inch of it. Her small hand couldn't even fit around the entire shaft, but it felt nice and warm as she stroked me from the base to the tip in a rhythm that was prob-ably playing in her head. I tried to control myself from moaning out loud, but the pre-cum that bubbled up on the tip of my dick put me on blast.

She moved her small body over between my legs, her juicy ass blocking my view from the TV as she bent over and took my dick into her mouth. Her ass jiggled as her body rocked, and my toes were curled so tight I thought I would spontaneously combust as I enjoyed the blessing her warm mouth provided. It wasn't long before I had unloosened her hair from her bun and grabbed a hold of her long tresses as her hair fell down around her face and across my lap, blocking my view of her mouth at work.

Shanyce was a pro at this shit though, and quickly moved her hair out of the way so that I could continue to watch. My baby was killing this shit. She knew just what to do to get me back in check.

"Yeah . . . suck my dick," I growled out as I pumped her face faster. I could feel my nut building up, and I wanted her to suck me bone dry. I would have to do the damn thing to her for this shit, because she went all out on this one.

The feel of her mouth working me out, and the smell of the chocolate candles she had burning on the dresser had me on tilt. Her hair felt like silk in my hands, and I brushed it away from her face so that I could watch my dick disappear between her full lips. She looked up at me briefly and winked her eye before taking me back in.

Something inside of me snapped and my body froze as I shot off in her mouth and she swallowed me up until every drop was out. I might just have to run her those two G's after all. Her head continued to bob up and down until I was worked up into another erection again. Shanyce was no damn joke, and I knew I kept her trouble-making ass around for a reason.

Vincent Clayton

Settin' Niggas Up

"Yo, you gave him the money?" I asked my man Choice while we blazed L after L at his spot. I liked Joey, I really did, but if this nigga wanted to really be put on, I had to have some dirt on him so that he wouldn't have a choice but to stay around. He didn't know I knew about the shit that happened with Shanyce's brother, but I made sure I got some head from that bitch often to make up for it. I put my man Choice on to that shit, too, because it was her damn fault anyway, and Choice didn't hesitate to bust her guts open every chance he got. Yeah, I knew it would fuck Street's head up if he knew, but that's the way the game is played, so fuck it. If he was on his game, we would be straight.

She ain't know that we got the pack back from her brother that same night either, but we didn't beat his ass like we wanted to, though. On the

strength of her, we just knocked him around a
little bit, enough to let him know we wasn't pla-
yin'. He was supposed to get the shit and bring
it back to us, but he tried to flip the script on
the plan. When one of our boys noticed that he
hadn't shown up when he was supposed to, Bird
caught his ass in a crack house in South Philly
tryin'a sell our shit.

"Yeah, he made it real easy to run that shit,
too, and I threw two more stacks on top for good
measure. I told him not to worry about paying
it back, though, he'd just owe me one," Choice
responded in his heavy Jamaican accent.

I nodded my head in agreement. "That's a
good look, nigga. As soon as he done runnin'
that money back, we gonna make good on that
promise, because you know he ain't gonna turn
all that shit in at once."

"I know, but that just makes it better for us.
We need to save that for something good. You
gonna up his rank, though?" Choice asked as he
flipped channels and coughed on blunt smoke,
stopping his search on a porn flick. I had to laugh
to myself because as much pussy as Choice got,
he loved watching pussy on the big screen even
more. These chicks in Philly loved dudes with
accents, and they fell all over Choice like he was
the only island nigga walking the city. Especially

them bitches from Bartram Village; they acted like he was God or something.

"Not just yet. I'ma have to let him sweat for the shit a little while first. He good, but he hasn't really proven himself to be more than a straggler. I mean, he doin' stick-ups with Bunz and shit." I laughed out loud, Choice following up behind me in agreement.

I actually took the time to read the newspaper article on what happened with Bunz and Street at that braid shop before New Year's. The media had been eating that shit up, too, trying to find out who the hell did it. The thing is, Lancaster Avenue was always poppin'. They had a better chance of Street bitchin' up and snitching than them finding out who did it. Black people don't tell shit, even if someone had indeed seen it all go down.

"He probably gonna holler at you about it, though. I know he said his chips were getting low."

"Yeah, well, we'll just have to make that nigga work extra hard for it. Put Bird on it. He'll have that nigga straight in no time."

Bird was another lieutenant that kept shit straight around here. He got the name Bird because that's exactly how he looked—like a black version of Big Bird and shit. He was a tall, light-

skinned black with a hawk nose and sharp fea-
tures that these bitches seemed to love, maybe
because he was always popping tags because he
stayed in the latest gear. He wasn't on no cup-
cake shit, though. That nigga would just as soon
dead you than argue the situation. Men, chicks,
and children; he didn't hesitate to pull the trigger. Not that him being that way was always
good, but when we needed him to handle business, handle business he did. "I'll holla at him
about it tomorrow."

"Cool. I gots to raise up. I got this fine-ass
chicken coming through tonight, and I got to
get my head on straight. She likes me working
on those tail feathers," I said to Choice, cracking
up because he knew how I felt about that anal
thing. This big-booty bitch named Brenda that I
fucked with every now and then loved anal sex,
and wouldn't let me get the pussy until I got with
her ass first. At times it could be a headache, but
fuck it. I just needed to get my dick wet, and I
was overdue.

"A'ight, my man. Stay gangsta."

"All day."

I jetted from Choice's crib in my champagne-
colored Jeep Explorer with the butterscotch
interior and dipped up Bala Cynwood, where I
laid my head. The only people that knew about

this spot were Choice and Bird, and even then they needed assistance in getting here. As much money as we were getting, I moved on, but them crazy niggas decided to stay in the hood to keep an eye on the action. Better them than me, because I needed to be able to close my eyes at night and not have to sleep with one eye open and both hands on my pistol.

Deading my lights before pulling up into the driveway, I did a quick sweep of my surroundings before exiting my vehicle. I had my hand on my 9 mm and one tucked on my waist, ready for action. I didn't really bring too many people out here, but you never know who's following you, and bitches stay tryin'a get a nigga, so I had to watch out for them too. Brenda was cool, but even the coolest ones always had some bright idea that never worked out.

I had about an hour before I had to pick up Brenda from in front of the Lord & Taylor located on City Line Avenue, so I took that time to get right before heading out.

I had my blindfold already in the car, and she knew the drill. I wouldn't even allow her to enjoy the scenery. Just in case she could see out the sides, I always went a different way and circled my block several times before actually going in, making the ride seem longer than it really was.

She couldn't even check the crib out. I only allowed her to take off the blindfold once we got up to my guest room, which she thought was my master bedroom because of the way it was laid out. Once we were done and rested a little bit, it was back to the blindfold until we got around the way. After doing a once-over around the crib, I did my little birdbath thing and jetted back out to meet Brenda. She was looking like a sexy little Popsicle when I pulled up, due to the wind and cold that snuck up on us a little while ago. No matter the weather, whenever I told her I was on my way, she always threw on that shit. She could have easily had on a warm bubble coat, but instead she had on a pair of fitted Sergio Valenté jeans that cupped her ass perfectly. The North Face ski jacket that stopped at her hips matched the leather knee boots with spiked heels that didn't keep her feet anywhere near warm. She was so hyped about the coat because Philly wasn't even up on them joints yet, and we had gone up to New York to get them.

She got in the car and immediately secured the blindfold around her eyes. I made sure it was tied tight before I pulled off. I turned the music up to the max, making it hard for her to concentrate on anything, and then did my usual, finally pulling up to the door.

Once inside, I set the alarm, and then I helped her upstairs to the room. At the top of the steps, she walked ahead of me, still blindfolded, like she knew exactly where to go. She didn't miss a beat, and didn't trip over a thing.

I closed and locked the door behind me before I settled on the bed, because you can never be too careful. Brenda immediately took the blindfold off, and walked over to me seductively, planting a soft kiss on my lips. I was ready to get it in, and the bulge in my pants let her know what time it was.

She backed up off of me and began a slow strip tease. I was pleasantly surprised to see that she didn't have a bra on, and her firm breasts sat up nicely. I licked my lips and pushed myself back on the bed, leaving my jeans at the bottom. I had taken everything out of my pockets and stuck the items in my coat, which was hanging on the back of the door. That way, if she tried to dig up in my pockets on the low, she would come up empty-handed. Not that she ever tried to get me before, but you just never know.

Her head game was to die for, and she wasted no time swallowing me. My eyes rolled up in the back of my head uncontrollably, and I pumped her face to the same rhythm she was sucking me. She was sloppy with the shit, just the way I liked it, and I grabbed a hold of her head to keep a steady pace. I knew her juices were flowing, and I couldn't wait to dig up in her, but I had to do what she wanted first. She lifted her head from my lap and slid a condom down with her mouth to protect us. Standing up on my bed with her back toward me, she squatted down and hovered over my erection, easing down onto me until she was comfortable. Surprisingly, her ass was tight, despite the fact that I was always tearing that shit up. I knew that I wasn't the only one she was sleeping with, and all them niggas got to tap it too.

She found her rhythm and bounced up and down on me, moaning all crazy and shit until she exploded. The girl was good at what she did, because in one motion, she set up off my dick, pulled the condom off, and replaced it with a fresh one, all before lying down on the bed with her legs up to her chest, ready for me to enter.

I'm not double-jointed, so I had to swing my legs around, almost hitting her in the head as I positioned myself to get in between her legs. Her walls had me gripped tight, too, and I lay down on top of her and rested my head between her breasts as I did the damn thing to her. Holding this nut was getting hard from her gripping and releasing my dick every time I pulled in or out, and I had to switch shit up before I crashed it.

I pulled out and lay down behind her, pulling her leg up and sliding in from the back, pounding away at her gushy pussy until I couldn't take it no more. The juice from inside of her was seeping out on the sides and coating my nuts like warm honey.

She would never let me cum inside of her, even though I had a condom on. Just when I was nearing my nut, she jumped up and snatched the condom off, milking my dick with her mouth until I went limp. None of that shit spilled out on the side or anything like that. Her skills were impeccable.

We chilled and snuggled up for about an hour before she got up and soaped up a warm rag to wash my dick. You know I laid my black ass back in the bed and let her take care of me, and by the time she came back to rinse the soap away, I was up and erect again, ready for more. She was ready to take care of me, too, but I had to get back to the hood to do this count on our supply. Brenda was a good girl, though, and didn't argue the fact like some of my past freaks had. She just got up off the bed, freshened herself up in the connecting bathroom, and put her gear back on, complete with blindfold and everything.

I did the same, sliding my coat back on at the last minute, and doing a once-over around the crib before I walked her from the bedroom and outside. I knew she would have freaked had she seen Goldie, one of the five Rottweilers I had guarding the house, approach us, but Goldie knew to keep shit quiet. She went and sat down in the corner as we left. They had food out, and I knew I would have to come back tomorrow to re-fill their bowls and clean up and stuff, so I made a note in my cell phone once we got in the car.

We were back to the hood in no time, and when we pulled up on her block, I slid her an envelope with her cash inside. Only after I prom-ised her a shopping spree in D.C. did she exit my Jeep and prance her sexy-ass up the steps and into her apartment building.

I rolled from there over to the spot to check out shit, and then I took my post on the block in the corner house. I had money to make, and I had to get some shit together for Journey to cook up tomorrow so that we could get this thing pop-pin'. It was going to be a good year. I could feel it.

Journey Clayton

Nickname: Me Coca-Cola

I was up bright and early the next day for school. Although I hadn't asked Vince if it was cool to set up my study date yet, I couldn't wait to see Khalid in class. The butterflies in my stomach danced around all crazy as I ate my small bowl of oatmeal and a piece of stale toast for breakfast; then I went in the room to hook my mom up before I left. Vince said he would take me shopping today, and even though I tried not to get my hopes up about it, I couldn't help but smile. I planned to ask him for a new pair of A. C. Greens and some Reebok Classics for school. I also wanted some jeans and panties and stuff too, so I would see how it all went down later on.

When I finally got my stuff together and got downstairs, I was pleasantly surprised to see Khalid waiting for me on the corner. I tried to hide my smile, but I couldn't when he smiled brightly at me. He embraced me in a tight hug when I neared him, and I fought the urge to keep my hold on him forever.

"Did you get all of your homework done? Those math problems were kind of hard," he said as he adjusted his hat on his head and tucked his scarf tighter into his coat.

We were learning the fundamentals of basic mathematics, and I was having a hard time keeping up with the geometry portion of the class. For a second I was embarrassed because I didn't have either a hat or a scarf, but he casually offered me his gloves, and looped his arm around mine before putting his hands inside of his coat. We stood outside talking for a while longer, until I finally asked why we were standing around.

"So, what are we waiting on?" I asked in a shy voice, wanting to start my walk so that I wouldn't be late for school. He had his dad to take him, but I couldn't walk as fast as a car, and if he wasn't walking with me, I needed to get going. I didn't just want to assume that I had a ride. "My dad is taking us."

Before I could respond, his dad, Joey, came out of the house dressed equally warm in a goose down coat that stopped at his waist, and a fresh pair of Timberland boots. He didn't even seem to care whether they got messed up in the snow and salt that covered the ground. I pulled my raggedy pea coat closer around my neck, making a mental note to hit Vince up for one of those later on as well.

"I can't get in the car with y'all. I'm not allowed to ride with strangers," I said to Khalid as I began to walk away.

"C'mon, it's cool. I'll let Vince know I dropped you off." Khalid's dad spoke in a frustrated voice. I eyed him suspiciously, partly because I didn't know if I could trust him, and for other reasons, including his attitude this early in the morning. He worked for my uncle; it ain't like he had a nine to five.

"Come on, Journey, it's cool. We only riding a few blocks anyway, and it's too cold out here to walk." I trusted him. Not sure why, but I did. Hesitating, I looked around at first to see who was out before I climbed into Joey's shiny black car and scooted over to make room for Khalid to sit down. Once we were inside and our seat belts were fastened, he reached over to grab my hand, and we held hands all the way to school in silence.

The view from the inside of the car looked totally different than the route I walked on a daily basis, rain or shine, and I took it all in, not knowing the next time I would be able to ride in this kind of luxury. The seats felt like they pulled you in and hugged you tight, and the interior smelled like cherry Kool-Aid, which I found out later was a car air-freshener shaped like a tree that you got from the car wash.

We pulled up to the school within minutes, and I wasn't exactly ready to get out of the warmth of Joey's car. Joey parked and got us out, ushering us into the school building. I quickly hung up my coat and took my seat in the class, taking the liberty of looking over my homework from the night before. I looked up just in time to see Khalid give his dad a hug before he slipped out of the building and Khalid took his seat. I didn't even get a chance to thank him.

Khalid smiled at me again before he pulled out his notebook to look over his homework as well. I wondered if he was nervous like I was, because I wasn't sure if I had gotten mine correct.

Mrs. Solomon wasn't in at all, so we had a substitute teacher that was off the chain. She wasn't dressed like the rest of the teachers in the school, who opted to dress more conservatively. Her form-fitting skirt that stopped just at her knees and made her butt look bigger than it probably was, was the first thing I noticed when she entered the classroom.

Her button-down shirt covered her perky breasts that threatened to bust through the fabric. It matched her shoes perfectly, and her three-inch stiletto heels gave her walk more *oomph* that everyone noticed. Her lip-gloss was poppin' too, and when she turned around to write her name on the chalkboard, I noticed that she had on a thong and not bloomers that showed your panty line through your clothes like the ones Mrs. Solomon wore. I remembered thinking I wanted to look just like her when I grew up, and I gave her my undivided attention for the rest of the day.

We played spelling games and did marathon math quizzes that had the girls competing with the boys, and before I knew it, it was time for lunch and recess. Even while we were in the cafeteria having our meal, everyone was hyped and bugged out over our new teacher and how much fun we were having. I missed Mrs. Solomon, but our substitute teacher, Ms. Reid, was on point, and she made learning our math lesson a lot of fun and easier to understand.

For the first time in never, I was actually having a good day in school, and we all got along. Even Gina and her stuck-up friends were being nice to me. We all played rope during recess, and even teamed up against the other girls in the class when we played Hangman, girls versus girls, and boys versus boys. Everything was looking up, and even when I noticed Gina pushing up on Khalid on the sly, I didn't even get mad because even though it wasn't official, he chose me, and that was all that mattered.

After school, he waited for me to get myself together in the classroom, and we walked out hand in hand, right past Gina and Marissa. Khalid didn't even appear to notice they were there. I looked back at Gina in time to catch the evil stare she threw my way, and I smiled back in return, letting her know she didn't faze me.

Our walk home was even more pleasant than the day before, and when we got to the block, I initiated the kiss before I ran off and went in the house.

When I walked in, Vince was already waiting inside, watching the ending of *Duck Tales*. I zoomed by, hung up my coat, and handled my business, making sure whatever dishes that the home health aide left were cleaned up.

On this day, Vince just gave me the Snow White, not making me beg for it or anything like that. I snatched the cap up from the table and took everything I needed, as well as my mom's food, into the room to get it over with. Usually I took my time with my mom, making sure that she was comfortable and all that, but today I had a mission to accomplish.

I fed her only half the food, which she took in pretty well, before I set up shop to give her what she needed. I had to take my time with this, though, making sure not to overcook the product, if you could actually do so. It took me a while to find a vein this time, and I almost lost hope until I saw a small vein pop up by her ankle that I was able to use. By the time I got done injecting her fix and had washed everything off, she was laid flat out on the bed. I turned the fan on low and fixed the covers around her, making sure the television was turned to Fox 29 before I left the room.

Vince was already at the door waiting for me, and I grabbed my coat and my house key, rushing behind him down the stairs before I lost sight of him. When I got outside, I jumped into the back seat of his Jeep, buckling my seat belt as he closed the door and jumped in himself. It was almost like he was driving a jet as we sped away and made our way to the Gallery to go shopping.

I had never been to the Gallery, but I knew that Gina's mom got her a lot of things from there, so I knew we were about to spend some money. We went into the Kids Foot Locker first, where I was able to pick out four pairs of sneakers and a pair of Timberlands like the ones I saw Khalid wear to school when it snowed.

I didn't even want Vince to help me with my bags after he paid for my stuff. I grabbed up the two bags the cashier put my stuff in and was out, ready to go to the next store.

We stopped in another shoe store, where Vince got himself some stuff before we went into Gymboree, a highpriced children's clothing store where I was able to pick out five outfits to go with my new shoes. I tried on all the clothes, too, making sure that everything fit, so that I wouldn't have to bring anything back. I settled on three pairs of jeans and two pairs of corduroy pants, with sweaters to match, before we left out.

I was content with what I had, but when he took me into the Children's Place clothing store and told me to get what I wanted, I almost passed out from the excitement. I took just as much time in there, piecing together my outfits. He reminded me to get some more underwear and undershirts and whatever else I needed before we left that store. I walked out of there with enough stuff to last me a month, mimicking the styles of clothes that I saw the other girls in my school wearing when we were allowed a dress-down day. Once we left there, we went into another shoe store, where I was able to get a nice pair of loafers and a pair of Mary Jane shoes that I had seen Gina and Marissa wear to school on occasions. Our last stop was the Gallery hair store, where I got like a hundred packs of barrettes and hair baubles. I didn't even know how to put them in, but I would figure it out before the week was out.

We went to McDonald's before we left there, and I started getting suspicious because I knew that for him to be spending this kind of money, he must want me to do something in return. I was quiet on the way back to the hood, still not believing my luck.

A half hour later, we pulled up in front of one of the apartment buildings in Bartram Village. I was scared because of the stories I heard about people being killed in the basements and stuff, and I refrained from even looking out the window, just in case I saw something I wasn't supposed to.

From my view in the back seat, I saw Vince talking to this big-booty girl on the stoop. She was all hugged up on my uncle like they really knew each other, and my young mind began to wander. If he had girls that looked like that all over him, what did he want with me? They conversed for a while longer before I saw Vince pull money from his pocket and hand it to the girl before beckoning me to get out of the car.

I was trying to grab all my stuff to bring it with me, but he told me to leave it all in the car except for the hair barrettes and stuff. I took the liberty of taking all of the clothing receipts out and putting them in my pocket before I went up to the strange girl. Vince told me to call him when I was finished getting my hair done. I looked skeptical about going, but I really didn't have a choice in the matter.

The hallway smelled like piss as we walked up to the third floor, and just like my teacher, I noticed this girl had on a thong too. That must have been the thing to have, because everybody was wearing them, and I made another mental note to get some of them next time I went out shopping with Vince.

Surprisingly, the girl's house was the bomb. She had a nice plush carpet that I couldn't step on until I removed my shoes. I was suddenly happy that I had put on clean socks that morning. From there we went straight to the kitchen, where she made me climb up on the sink and lay flat down so that my head could hang over the edge inside of the bowl. She loosened my hair from my raggedy ponytail; then she took a big plastic juice pitcher from the cabinet and filled it with warm water to pour over my hair. I used my shirt to cover my eyes as she washed and scrubbed my hair several times before finally applying some conditioner and combing it through with a wide-toothed comb. My hair felt silky and smooth, and after she combed and rubbed every follicle, she rinsed me out and wrapped my hair in a towel, instructing me to have a seat in one of the kitchen chairs that surrounded the table.

She left the room for a few minutes, but came back with a hair dryer and a few other items that she would need to get the job done. I listened to her yap away on the phone, telling whomever she was talking to how all the niggas out there were foul and that even though Vince broke her off with good dick and some cash every so often, she wasn't his girl. I just giggled to myself as she roughly dried my hair and sectioned it off into two small parts before corn rowing my hair in a zigzag pattern. She hung my barrettes from the ends.

My hair easily reached the center of my back, and the barrettes clapped together as I walked into the bathroom to look at the new me. I was pleasantly surprised at the girl I saw in the mirror. My hair was nice and shiny and long, hanging down my back, making my face look different.

She came in the bathroom and smiled at me smiling at myself, saying something to me for the first time today. "You like it?"

"Yes. Thank you so much."

"No problem." She instructed me on how to take care of my hair. "Just keep a scarf on it every night, and try not to scratch too much, and you should be good for at least two weeks."

"I don't have a scarf," I replied. I had forgotten to get one from the hair store. After all, I really didn't know what to buy, since I wasn't really into the hair care thing. "I got one. Don't worry about it."

I left the bathroom just in time to see Ms. Reid, my substitute teacher, walk into the apartment. She smiled at me when she came in, calling me by my name when she spoke.

I was shocked that she recognized me because I didn't really recognize the new me that I saw in the mirror.

"Hi, Ms. Reid," I spoke back shyly before looking down at my hands. She was even prettier up close, and I couldn't believe she lived right around the way. We held a brief conversation before the girl that was doing my hair came back into the living room, heated at whomever she was talking to on the phone.

"See, Journey, a man ain't good for nothing but giving you what you need to maintain. You're a pretty girl. Just keep yourself nice and clean, and keep your gear together, and you'll have a man eating out the crack of your ass for the rest of your life."

"Toya, what kind of advice is that to give a growing girl?" Ms. Reid said, shaking her head and smiling at Toya, introducing her to me as her sister. I took in that tad bit of information, though, just in case I needed it down the line. I had a feeling that this year was going to be my year, and I knew I would have to stay on Vince if I wanted my shit to stay tight.

Vincent Clayton

Big Things Poppin'

"You ready?" I spoke into the phone when I noticed Toya's number pop up. She took a lot longer with Journey's hair than I thought she would, but that was cool. It gave me time to set up shop at the crib so that Journey could get to cooking this good coke up. I just got some new shit from my connect that I wanted to test out, and I needed to see how Journey would do with my sister-in-law before I put it out on the street.

"Yeah, she ready. Hurry up, nigga," Toya spoke into the phone before banging on me. She was mad because I wouldn't let her suck my dick, but in reality, she needed to up her head game if we were gonna roll like that.

I ain't sweat that shit, though. I just went ahead and got my niece, pulling up to the door and beeping the horn, not bothering to call upstairs for her to come out. Much to my surprise,

Toya's sister, Tyfanie, walked Journey out to the car. She was the shit, and wasn't tryin'a give a nigga no play whatsoever. She wasn't stuck up or nothin', but I guess her being a teacher had a lot to do with how she dealt with people. I ain't give a fuck about none of that, though. I'd bend her ass right over the back of the couch right next to her damn sister and fuck the shit out of both of them. Just thinking about it made my dick hard.

Toya did a good job with Journey's hair, making her look like a well-kept young lady. It almost made me feel bad about what I was doing to her . . . almost. Shit, she'd have to learn how to maintain eventually. I was just showing her the ropes.

Journey quickly climbed into my Jeep and shut the door, buckling her seat belt as we drove off. I already told Choice and Bird that I would be out later, not bothering to tell either one of them what I had cooking up. I didn't want too many people in my shit, just in case it didn't work out the way I planned.

We pulled up to the crib in less than five minutes, and I saw the look on Journey's face when she didn't see all of her bags in the back seat where she'd left them. I knew enough about her to know she wouldn't ask for the shit either; she'd look upstairs first. I had the bags hidden in my sister-in-law's room for the time being. I needed her to cook this shit up before she even touched her homework, and she needed to understand that shit didn't come for free. I spent well over a thousand dollars on her earlier, and she would have to work that off.

When we got in the crib, she ran right into her room, expecting her bags to be on her bed, or at least in the closet. I took a seat at the table and pulled the brick out of my pocket, allowing her to search around a little before she came back to me.

"Uncle Vince," she said to me in a strained voice, like she was trying to keep herself from crying. I ain't give a fuck, though. By the time I was done with her, she wouldn't have a tear left in her damn body. Crying is for weak bitches, and she would be a soldier whether she wanted to be or not.

"Yeah, wassup, Journey?" I asked her as if I didn't know what she was looking for. I probably should have felt bad about what I was doing to her, and I could see her little nose getting red and her eyes starting to well up as she blinked back tears. She had to learn that she couldn't trust anyone, though. Not even herself.

"What happened to the stuff you bought for me? Did you take it back to the store?"

"I might have. Why?" I asked, looking her in the face and trying not to smirk. She was falling apart, but in a month from now, nothing would faze her.

"Because I have all of the receipts right here," she said, pulling a handful of receipts from her pocket. I laughed a little because she was at least smart enough to know that I couldn't get my money back without them. She was a little brighter than I thought.

"Did you think I needed those to return your stuff?"

"Yeah."

"Well, I didn't. Now, this is what I need you to do. . . ." I started her off with just cooking down enough for five or six tops at a time, to make sure she didn't mess up. "Measure out the baking soda in individual scoops for each one, so that you don't add too much. And don't spill any of the product."

I showed her how to use the scale for measuring and how to pack the product into the vials. Her hands were a bit shaky at first, but once she got a rhythm going, she was knocking them joints out without much effort. Once she made up about thirty tops, I had her do the ultimate test to see if she had done it correctly. "Go give this to your mother."

"Now? I already gave her what she needed for today."

"Journey, you want your stuff back, right?" I asked her with a serious expression on my face. It took her forever to cook up that little bit of shit, and even though I told my people that I wouldn't be out until later, it was getting too damn late for me to still be inside. "Yes, I want my stuff back."

"Then you know what you need to do." She hesitantly got up from the table and went into the room to test the product on her mother. I stood in the doorway and watched as she approached my sister-in-law, who was up watching the news. Journey told her that she was going to be giving her another hit, and she happily obliged. I just hoped this simple bitch didn't overdose, but it had been a couple hours since her earlier hit, so she would probably be cool.

Journey was very meticulous in how she set everything up, being sure to wash her hands and everything before she touched the supplies. My sister-in-law could hardly contain herself as she waited for Journey to get her situation right. Journey knew her shit, too, taking her time to find the vein and everything. If she kept up this shit here, I might have to put her on the block.

I took a seat in the living room and waited impatiently for her to finish up. I knew my brother didn't really want his wife strung out like that, but she was a grown-ass woman that made a grown-ass decision. I was just helping her out. When Journey came back out, I showed her how to clean up all traces of activity, sliding back into my sister-in-law's room to hide the rest of my supply and get Journey's shit out of the closet.

"Here's your stuff. Keep doing what I need you to do, and I'll keep lacing you like this. Understood?" She didn't open her mouth to respond; she just shook her head. Peeking in the room one more time, I saw that my sister-in-law was feeling nice, and I knew that Journey had done a good job cooking this shit up. Normally I would have gotten at least some head from Journey, but it was already getting late and I'd already stressed the girl out, so I let her slide. When I came back into the living room, she was undressed and waiting on the couch with her hair tied up in a scarf. My dick jumped at attention, and I almost doubled back, but I kept it moving.

"Journey, go to bed. I'll be back tomorrow so that you can package up some more shit. Come straight home from school."

"Okay, but what do I do for my mom in the morning? I used my last one earlier."

I reached into my pocket and gave her two caps of Snow White from the bag I had earlier today. The stuff that she had just cooked up would be given out as testers, and we would be doing that for the next few days to see how it went over. If our clientele was demanding it, we would go with the new connect.

I slid over to Choice's place to put him on to what I was trying to do. Just as I had asked, he had two fiends waiting on the corner for me when I got there. We walked down to one of our hit spots on the block and gave the fiends one top each, to go with what they had just purchased, to get the party started. The one dude, Smitty, was a lifelong customer, and every time we got some new shit we would hook him up, because he sent a lot of traffic our way.

"Smitty, let me know how you like this, man. I'll hook you up if you keep sending traffic my way. You know how we do."

Smitty just shook his head and moved the party upstairs, not even bothering to ask any questions. Me and Choice went back on the block so that we could get things poppin'.

"So, that's the new shit?" Choice asked me as he puffed his L and leaned against the side of the bar. He was the one that put me on to the connect, and I knew once I told him what I had cooking up, he'd be in.

"Yeah. My plan is to put Street on the project so that he could get his game up. I only had like thirty tops made up, but over the next couple of days and over the weekend, we'll just pass out samples to see how it goes over." "You think Street ready for this game, man?"

"Yeah, I think he is. The question is does he think he's ready?"

My plan was to up Joey's status within the next couple of months, but I needed to get this dude on some shit that would have him stuck for good. That reminded me that I needed to see Shanyce about some shit too. It was about time for her to ride this dick if she wanted her little boy to make it another day.

It wasn't until three in the morning when I finally got home, and I was tempted to creep back up around the way to take Journey up on that offer from earlier. I swear that girl gave the best head ever. Instead, I stroked my nut up until I busted all over my legs and shit, not even bothering to wipe the shit up.

Rolling over, I closed my eyes and called it a night, knowing I would have to be up in a few hours to start my grind again. This was going to be my year. I could feel it. But at the same time, shit was going too smooth, and something was telling me that the shit with Bunz wasn't over.

I would have to pay that nigga a visit before he ran up on us. After all, he was a stick-up kid, and they would take from their own momma, so why would my team be exempt?

Joey Street

Peepin' 'round Corners

I started running that money back to Vince on the low, but something just didn't feel right. I mean, he never inquired about the late payments or anything. Choice ran that cash too quickly for me as well. It wasn't suspect because he's looked out before, but that shit just didn't sit right with me. I didn't question it, though; I just got back out there on my grind so that I could build my stash back up. I had the payback money from Choice, so I was in the clear, but I needed some dough so that I could sit comfortably for a while and not stress.

In the midst of all that, I opened up a savings account in my son's name so that I wouldn't have to keep so much money in the crib. That way, if I went down for some shit, the feds couldn't freeze up my funds. I had my mom as the other person on the account so that they wouldn't be wondering how thousands of dollars were being deposited on a weekly basis.

I didn't think I was going to be in the game for much longer. It wasn't intuition; it was fear, because I just felt like some dumb shit was about to happen.

Vince told me to stick around on the block today because he wanted to holler at me about some new shit he and Choice had come up with. If it was about making more than I was now, I was definitely going to be there. I just felt like my time was limited. You ever have that feeling like somebody is watching you and shit? Like you're going to turn the corner and something or somebody is gonna jump out on you? I wasn't watching my back or nothing, but I stayed strapped because my gut was tight about some shit, and I couldn't put my finger on why just yet.

After I dropped my little man and Vince's niece off at school, I went and handled some business that ran me until like two-thirty in the afternoon, and then I copped me some breakfast from this joint down the bottom on Lancaster Avenue called Texas Weiner across the street from that braid shop we got before New Year's. I felt funny even pulling up around there because that shit brought back unwanted memories, but they had these spicy breakfast sausages and hot cakes to die for. I just hoped I wouldn't have to die literally. When I walked up into the store, I stood to the side because it was always packed like crack up in this joint no matter what time of day you got there. Since they only stayed open until about three in the afternoon anyway, you had to get in when you could fit in, or you missed out until six the next morning.

I placed my order with one of the waitresses. Out of the corner of my eye, I couldn't help but notice this dude in the cut near the back of the store mean-mugging me the entire time I was standing there. I gave cutie my order and ice-grilled his ass right back, tucking my chain on the low inside of my sweatshirt, just in case I had to lay a nigga down and jet.

I leaned up against the wall, wondering where I had seen this cat before. Did we have beef? I barely came down here except to get something to eat when I wanted a good breakfast, and with the exception of New Year's Eve, I didn't even travel in these parts. Maybe he was from around the way and was on the same mission I was. Bartram Village is full of clown-ass niggas trying to come up; that's where Bunz was from.

I checked my hip for my shit, and kept it grizzly. This spot was packed too tight for him to pull out on me, but just in case he was a nigga like Bird that didn't care who was there, I stayed on alert.

The waitress gave him his food before I got mine, and I was tempted to leave. I didn't want this dude to have one up on me because he was able to leave and go get his boys; but I wasn't about to jet like I was a scared nigga, either. He paid for his food and a fresh squeezed orange juice and slid on down my end, since there was only one way in and one way out. I gave him just enough room to slide by without brushing against me, but he stopped at the door and looked back. "Hey, tell Shanyce I said wassup," he said with a smirk on his face that I was close to knocking the fuck off. Who was he, one of her exes or some shit?

"I certainly will. Who should I say asked about her?" I asked with the same smirk, letting this man know that what he said didn't faze me nearly as much as he thought. Shanyce ain't no fool; trust me on this one.

"Tell her, her Monday man said wassup. I'll see her next week."

Just when I was going to snap, the waitress called me over to get my platter. In that split second when I looked away and looked back, he was gone. To say I was heated was putting it mildly, but I paid for my shit and gave her a tip before

I left, checking my surroundings at the door before walking to my whip. *Her Monday man, huh? I'm not going to even question her about that shit right this second. I need to investigate first.*

That shit ruined my damn appetite for the moment, so I slid the food in my passenger seat and took it back around the way, promising to devour that shit later. Hitting up Choice, he told me that the crew was at his spot, so I just went over there to see what the transition would be. I had paper to get; that's all that mattered at this point.

I walked in on Choice, Vince, and Bird passing several lit blunts around while they watched game highlights on ESPN. I took a seat next to Choice on the sofa and jumped into the rotation until they were ready to talk. I was still on steam from that earlier bullshit, but they would never know it. You don't tell your left hand what your right hand is doing all the time.

Once we got caught up on what was good in the sports world, Choice turned to the news and put the television on mute so that we could talk. I could read lips, so I kept watching television while we talked, just in case some shit happened that I needed to know about. There was a funeral last week for that woman that Bunz killed, and the news was still riding that shit like it just happened today, not a few weeks ago.

"So, I got this new product from them Miami niggas that's like Snow White to the tenth
power," Vince spoke between puffs on his L. No
matter who we got our product from, we always
marketed the shit as Snow White to keep the
customers coming back. We always tried to get
some better shit than we had the last time, because we were always in transition to step the
game up to the next level.

"Did we start putting it out yet?" I asked, di-
verting my attention away from the TV for a quick
second to join the conversation. They weren't
talking anything of significance on TV anyway;
just the same shit from yesterday that we already
heard about.

"Yeah, we started passing out samples over
the weekend, and they asking for the shit like
crazy. We just need to decide if we're going to go
with this new connect or not," Bird said before
he started choking on blunt smoke. The shit we
were puffing on was the truth, and I had to put it
down if I wanted to get some shit accomplished
today.

For the life of me, I couldn't figure out why I
was the only soldier here on this meeting. Maybe
they were about to up my rank or some shit, because normally these meetings were only held
amongst Vince, Choice, and Bird. Hustle boys

had an entirely different meeting involving the product. I didn't say a word because I didn't want to assume that I was in, but if they had me there, it must have been something up.

"Okay, well, let's get this money," I said, trying to sound hype about the shit. In reality, I wanted to wild the fuck out on Shanyce's dumb ass, but I'd deal with her later.

"Yo, Street, we wanna put you on to some real cash, but we don't all feel like you've really put up the effort to prove you were down. How many bodies you got on you now?" Vince asked through the haze of thick smoke that circled us like storm clouds. What was this nigga tryin'a get at? He knew I was down for the crew at the drop of a hat.

"Like six? Why you ask?" I asked nervously, my high completely blown. They were testing me, this I knew, and if I wanted to stay on, I knew what was coming next. There wasn't any bowing out, though. It was kill or be killed in this game. I just had to decide which way I wanted to go.

"Because real killers don't hesitate. We got a situation we need you to handle," Bird said through choking. I wanted to tell that nigga to put the L down and get his head on straight, but I kept the thought to myself.

"What's the situation?" I asked, turning my head to the television just in time to see Bunz's dumb ass being wrestled to the ground by some angry cops. What the fuck was this nigga up to now?

I grabbed the remote and hit the sound so that I could hear what was going on, causing the conversation to pause as we all turned to the news. I was looking because I wanted to make sure this incident wasn't in direct relation to the New Year's Eve shit. Bunz's dumb ass would straight drop a dime on me if it meant his own freedom. That's why I was kicking myself in the ass now because I did that stick-up with him.

He was trying to hide his face from the camera once he was up from the ground. Apparently he tried to rob the Chinese store and got caught. That was the most asinine shit I heard all day. How are you trying to rob a Chinese store and they behind glass? I swear he never fails to amaze me.

"We need you to handle a situation," Choice said, snatching the remote from my hand and turning the television off. These niggas meant business and were obviously trying to give me more stripes. Who was I to argue with their decision?

"Okay, what you need me to do?"

They all got up and instructed me to follow them into the back room of Choice's apartment. I'd never walked around his place to this extent, with the exception of using the bathroom and going to the kitchen. The door was locked, and Choice searched his pockets for the key to open it so that we could go in. When the door opened, I smelled the stench of old blood and alcohol, and I figured they wanted me to ditch a body. I ain't give a fuck; I'd just roll that nigga up in a carpet and he'd be floating on the Schuylkill by midnight.

They were all in front of me so I couldn't see who it was, but when I finally got in the room, I was floored when I saw Shanyce's brother tied to a chair, looking like a bloody mess but still breathing. I wondered briefly if they found out that he stole that pack from me, but nothing was ever said.

"Like I said, we have a situation," Bird said after closing the bedroom door. I didn't know what they wanted me to do, but I knew I would have to take it to my grave. I'd regret this later on, but my loyalty was to the crew first. I'd just have to deal with the guilt at a later date.

Journey Clayton

The Kissing Game

I was finally able to convince Vince to let me study with Khalid. It was awkward at first because I couldn't really explain to Khalid why we always had to be at his house. I just told him that my mom was sick and my uncle didn't want people in the house. It wasn't a total lie, but it wasn't the complete truth either. Besides, his mom gave us snacks and let us study in the room with the door closed. I guess she trusted her son to not try anything crazy.

We spent a good amount of time studying, because in addition to learning spelling and arithmetic, we were required to decipher passages from the Bible as well. Khalid really knew his stuff, and could recite every book of the Bible in order, frontwards and backwards. I always got stuck after Deuteronomy, but I was getting better at it.

On this particular day, we were lying side by side on beanbags, talking about what we wanted to be when we grew up. I was not really surprised by too many things, given the situation that I was in, but Khalid always caught me off guard. That was one of the many things I liked about him.

"I think I want to be President of the United States when I grow up," Khalid said whimsically as he lifted his legs to the ceiling and lowered them back to the ground like we had done in gym class earlier. I was keeping count on my own, but my legs got tired long before his did. "The president? I think you should go for it."

"I plan to, and you can be the first lady, because you know the president has to have a wife."

"That means we would have to get married," I threw in there just to see what he would say. Was he implying that I would be a part of his future?

"I plan to wife you, since you already my girl. When we get older, we might as well make it official."

I looked at his dimples while he smiled and continued talking, not believing my luck. He could choose from any girl in the class and he chose me. I couldn't help but smile as I brushed my braids away from my face so that they could rest on the side of the beanbag. He had me smiling all day when he complimented me on my hair first thing in the morning. That was two weeks ago, and it was just starting to get a little fuzzy from me scratching between my cornrows. Vince said I would be able to get it done again over the weekend, so I really wasn't worried about it.

Khalid was no longer hiding our friendship from the other girls in the class, either, allowing me to wear his gold *K* chain that his dad got him for his birthday last year. He even carried my books into the school and home from school. During recess, he always made sure I was cool before he went to play with the boys, and checked on me periodically until it was over. I didn't really know what love was, but it had to be what I felt about Khalid. I wouldn't know what to do without him.

I wanted to tell him about the things my uncle made me do to him, but I didn't want him to feel sorry for me, or even worse, not like me anymore. Instead, I just kept smiling—and it came naturally, because he made me feel so good on the inside. He could talk forever about all of his dreams for the future, and I'd follow him to the moon. He said we would be together forever, and I believed him.

"Journey, you daydreaming again?" Khalid said, flashing me that gorgeous smile. He had dimples so deep you could put your finger in them, and I hoped if we ever had children, our son would inherit them.

"You caught me," I slyly laughed as I turned my attention back to him. He was now sitting up on the beanbag with his legs folded Indian-style. I sat up and matched his position, scooting my beanbag closer so that we could hold hands.

"What do you know about kissing?" he asked me with a devilish look on his face.

"Not much besides what we do. Why?"

"Because I was looking at one of my dad's movies, and we can take kissing to another level."

I was intrigued. All we ever did was mash our lips together for a few seconds before pulling away. That in itself made me blush, so I couldn't begin to imagine what else there was to do. My mom and dad were always high from smoking marijuana before they turned to harder stuff, from what I can remember from back in the day. I couldn't recall any public displays of affection, so I just had to trust him. I felt bad because I knew the things that my uncle made me do with my mouth were not good, but how could I tell Khalid that?

"Okay, give me your hands and move closer," Khalid instructed, and I unfolded my legs and scooted closer, folding them again so that our knees touched. I placed my now trembling hands in his and waited for what I was supposed to do next.

"Now close your eyes and do to me what I do to you."

I closed my eyes nervously and waited for him to continue. He started off by kissing my lips like we normally did, and my grip on his hands got tighter during contact. I felt him trying to part my lips with his tongue. I was hesitant to open my mouth, doing so only slightly, so that he could slip his tongue in. My eyes were shut tight as I softly sucked on his tongue, tasting the remnants of the pineapple Now and Laters that we were eating moments before. I could feel a pulse in my panties that made me jump back and open my eyes. I was holding his hands so tight it felt like I was crushing them, but he looked back at me and smiled.

"How was that?" he asked me before standing up from where we were sitting.

"I don't know. I liked it. How should it have been?"

"I liked it too, but don't worry; we'll get plenty of practice. I got something I want to show you."

I thought he was about to pull his dick out or something, and I wasn't quite ready for all that yet. I was already kind of confused about the things I did with Khalid thus far, because it felt totally different from what my uncle made me do. I hated my uncle touching me, and I didn't necessarily love Khalid touching me either, but for some reason, I felt I could trust him and he wouldn't hurt me.

I was ready to protest when he turned and walked to the closet. I thought maybe he was going to show me a new shirt or some sneakers that his dad just bought him, but what he turned around with surprised me even more.

"Khalid, where did you get that from?" I said, jumping up from my sitting position on the floor and moving to the other side of the bed. Khalid held a broad smile on his face as he handled the shiny chrome on the .22 he was holding. I didn't know what to expect, but a gun damn sure wasn't on the top of my list. I recognized the type of gun immediately because it looked similar to the one my uncle had hidden under my mother's bed that I wasn't supposed to know about.

"It's my dad's. He doesn't know that I'm up when he's trying to hide his stash. This ain't the only thing he got in here."

I walked up to the closet and stood to the side as Khalid showed me the sliding panel in the wall inside of his closet. It held ridiculous amounts of money and vials stuffed with Snow White, which

I recognized from my house. On the weekends, Vince had me cooking and bagging up product for his crew until the wee hours of the morning, and I swear I was having nightmares of white tops chasing me down the street.

"I think you should put that up before your mom walks in," I said to Khalid, backing away from the closet and staying clear of what I just saw. I ain't want no parts of that, and that's why I had to keep my mouth shut. He could never know what part I played in the game.

"Awww, what? You scared of this little gun?" Khalid said while imitating moves from shows he'd seen on TV. I was ducking because I didn't want to get shot accidentally.

"Khalid, stop playing before that thing goes off. Put it up," I pleaded from my position across the room. I'd seen on the news too many times how some unsuspecting child was killed from playing with a gun, and I wasn't ready to go just yet.

"It's not even loaded. See," he said, walking toward me. Just then, the door opened and Ms. Shanyce, Khalid's mom, was standing in the doorway, holding a plate of fresh-baked cookies.

"Boy, what are you doing with that? Where did you get a gun from?"

Ms. Shanyce rushed into the room, snatching the gun from Khalid's hands, dropping the plate of cookies in the process. She was shaking and crying, and I understood, because I was scared myself as I tried to hide on the other side of the bed just in case it went off.

She snapped for a quick second, cursing up a storm and bringing us into the living room. She sat us down and asked Khalid a million times where the gun had come from. He told her he found it, but I knew he was just protecting his dad. He didn't mention the other stuff he had in the closet, either, and I didn't say a word. I just sat back and tried not to cry, because I knew that Khalid had messed up and I wouldn't be able to see him for a while except for when we were in school.

She was still going off after she walked away, consistently dialing Khalid's dad and getting his voice mail. She was cursing him out, leaving message after message, telling him he needed to get home. Khalid just sat with his hands folded tightly in his lap, never taking his gaze away from the floor. I wanted to hold him and tell him it would be cool, but I knew it wouldn't be. Mr. Joey would be in trouble as well, and I just hoped that didn't trickle down to me.

After what seemed like forever, Ms. Shanyce instructed me to get my coat on so that she could walk me home. Khalid had to come too, because there wasn't anyone there to watch him, but the entire time we walked, she was cursing him out and promising an ass whipping when they got back. We normally held hands when we walked, but today we had to walk on either side of his mom, and I missed him already. I still had my first real kiss, though, and I held on to that as we made the trip around the corner.

I went up the steps, and she watched until I closed the door. I could still hear her cursing Khalid out as they walked away. I ran up the steps and looked out the window, hoping he would glance back once more, but by the time I got upstairs, I could see them turning the corner.

After taking care of my mom and looking over my homework once more, I went ahead and called it a night. I would find out what happened with Khalid at school tomorrow, but tonight, I had my kiss. I didn't have to deal with Vince tonight, either, so that just made it even sweeter.

Vincent Clayton

Snitches Dig Ditches

"Yo, what's all this about?" Joey asked with fear in his eyes.

I knew this nigga was pussy, but my plan was to shake that shit out of his ass today. Real killers don't give a fuck, and he needed to learn how to take the emotion out of it. We was going to make him our ditch man, if he could just get his head on straight. He would hesitate to pull a trigger, but when it came to covering his tracks, he never left footprints. "This here is a snitch nigga, and a thief on top of that. Ain't that right, Sanchez?" I said, speaking to Shanyce's brother. His name wasn't really Sanchez; we just called him that because he looked like he could be Puerto Rican or Dominican. We fucked him up real nice, and with the combination of dope we fed his ass, he couldn't lift his head from his chest even if he tried.

It was time to dead that nigga. We let him slide a little when he didn't follow directions with stealing the pack from Joey, but this dude just kept doing stupid shit, like taking money off the top, even though we paid him good to set niggas up for us. We were hooking him up with supply when he did shit for us, on top of what he copped, and he was still acting a fool.

"Well, what this got to do with me?" Joey was shaking at this point, and it made me wonder how he managed to get six bodies under him if he couldn't even get his heart straight.

"You tryin'a earn more stripes, right? You ready to step the game up?" I asked him while I sparked up another Dutch. I was prepared to give him a lead position if he acted right, but he wasn't ready for lieutenant status just yet. He still didn't have enough heart, and we needed to fix that situation with Bunz immediately.

"Yeah, nigga, but damn. He family."

"And what does that mean to you?"

The situation got intense immediately, because he knew he wasn't going to be able to back out or it would be his head next. I didn't have a problem passing Sanchez the gun to dead this nigga. That just meant that Sanchez got to live for a few more hours.

Moving my attention from him to my hip, I felt my phone vibrate against my side. Taking a quick peek, I saw that it was Shanyce calling. That was cool, because I planned to stop by there anyway.

"So, what's it gonna be, nigga? You disposing this body today or what?" Bird asked him as he paced back and forth. Bird didn't have a lot of patience when it came to bullshit, and if it was up to him, Sanchez would have been deaded last night when we first brought that nigga here, instead of waiting on Street to show up. "Gimme the gwap."

I gave Street a brand new nine and stepped outside of the room. I didn't need to witness the shit; I just needed it to go down.

Taking a seat in front of the TV, I noticed that Street's phone was vibrating on the table. Picking it up, I noticed it was Shanyce calling again. Some shit must have gone down for her to be calling both of us, because she barely called my phone, except when she was looking for Joey or to confirm when I was coming through for that payback. A small part of me thought she enjoyed the dick-down even though she tried to act like she ain't want to give it to me. Just thinking about that shit made my dick hard.

"Yo, y'all niggas handle this. I'll check in with y'all later on." I peeked into the room before I left. Joey's ass was still standing there with the gun, and Bird and Choice was leaning against the windowsill, waiting for this simple nigga to make a move. I knew he would be in there for a good while, so I decided to slide on over to see Shanyce about some shit. Street lived within walking distance, so I left my Jeep parked in front of Choice's crib and let my feet carry me around the block. My watch read six, which was about right, because Street's simple ass didn't show up until damn near four o'clock. I wondered briefly if my niece had made it home yet, because I knew she studied with Street's son. I didn't need her to be there when I got there, but that was a chance I was willing to take.

I had turned Joey's phone off before I left because I needed him to concentrate on getting rid of that body. Whatever Shanyce wanted could wait until he was done handling his business, since it was too early to be moving a body out anyway. It was dark outside at this time of day, true that, but it would be too many witnesses, and we didn't need that nigga getting caught up in no rush hour traffic or some bullshit like that.

I knocked on the door a few minutes later, and I could hear Shanyce going off on somebody on

the phone. I knew it wasn't Street because neither Bird nor Choice would be letting that nigga
use the phone until this time tomorrow.

When she answered the door, she was surprised to see me, of course, and ended her call
immediately. It was probably her nosey-ass sister, Rita. I would bang that bitch, too, if she let
me.

"What you doing here, Vince? And where is
Joey? Why he not answering his phone?" she
said as she stood in the doorway acting like she
wasn't going to let me in.

"I got him handling something for me. He'll be
here before the sun comes up."

"Well, I need him to handle a situation with
his son now."

"He'll be here, but as of right now, I need you
to handle a situation."

"I just told you I'm having a situation with my
son," she said with way too much attitude, while
making the space between her and the door
smaller.

"As if today ain't payback. Is Joey here right
now to handle it?" I asked while I walked up the
steps to stand in the doorway with her. "No, he's
not, but—"

"Then you need to be sucking my dick then."
She looked defeated as she took the opportunity

to look both ways down the street before letting me in. I didn't give a fuck who saw me go inside because on some real shit, half the neighborhood knew what Street's bedroom looked like. That's what you get when you try to turn a whore into a housewife. She just happened to get knocked on Street, and that's how it went down. Shit, I remember back in the day when we was young boys playing "catch a girl, get a girl" and we ran trains on her ass every Friday. Southwest niggas been beating that pussy up for years.

She walked ahead of me, and on the way up, she went toward her son's room. I walked straight to the bedroom, since I knew where it was, and stripped down to my socks before I sprawled out on their plush-ass comforter. She had candles and shit all over the place, and just thinking about the shit she did with her mouth had my dick pointing to the ceiling. I knew she was checking on her seed, and I needed her to hurry that shit up so I could get back on my grind.

When she finally came into the room, she slammed the door shut and locked it. I ain't give a fuck; I was too busy stroking my dick to think about the shit. I just needed her to get her jaw working so I could bust this nut. I did chance a look at her while she was getting undressed, and

I have to admit that Shanyce was still the shit, even after carrying Khalid.

She had a nice heart-shaped ass that might have had Beyoncé jealous if she wasn't Beyoncé. Her breasts still sat up perky, and her nipples looked like dark chocolate kisses. She climbed on the edge of the bed and crawled toward me with a sexy scowl on her face that let me know that, true, she was mad at me, but she missed the dick.

"Yeah, you missed Big Daddy, didn't you?" I asked her as she replaced my hand with her mouth and deep-throated me down to my balls. Shanyce was the truth, because although I didn't have a yard, I had a smooth ten that had circumference like a muthafucka. She took that shit like her last name was Hoover, and had me gritting my damn teeth and curling my toes, trying to hold this nut down.

Watching Shanyce's ass rock back and forth had me hypnotized, and I had to get my head on straight before I crashed it. This bitch was like a snake charmer, and I was a python swaying back and forth to her rhythm. I love a sloppy blowjob, and the sound of her slurping my balls and licking the vein on the underside of my dick had me on tilt for real.

I pumped her face a few more times before I gently pulled my dick from her mouth and pulled her on top of me. I wasn't worrying about a damn condom because she lived at the clinic, and my cousin Tisha that worked there always made sure I got her test results. Her pussy felt extra warm as she slid down on me, and for someone who had an attitude with me, her pussy was awfully wet.

"Damn, girl, this shit is right," I said to her as I held her by her small waist and pounded up into her. Her titties bounced around freely, and I was enjoying the view. She leaned forward, slowing me down, and grinded her pussy down on my dick in a hard, slow grind that had my eyes positioned on the back of my head immediately. Damn, she was going for broke on this one.

She was doing the damn thing to me, kissing on the side of my neck and sucking my lips into her mouth like she loved me and shit. She hand-fed me her nipples while she bounced on me, and I was so close to cumming inside of her I was about to lose it. When she leaned back, she bounced on me real hard and placed her hand around the base of my dick, stroking me while she fucked me. That shit blew my mind because that was a technique I only saw porn stars do.

"Damn, bitch, I'm about to cum," I said to her in a strained voice as my cum threatened to shoot to the top of my dick and spit out of the head.

She worked her stroke faster until the very last second, when she hopped off of me and used her mouth to create a seal around the head of my dick. She sucked the cum from my dick like she was siphoning air from an oxygen tank. I blasted off in her mouth so hard my body raised up off the bed a little bit, and it felt like my heart stopped for a second. She continued to milk my dick until I couldn't possibly cum anymore, and she stood up and wiped her mouth off with an angry look on her face.

"Put your shit on and let yourself out, nigga," she said as she walked toward the connecting bathroom. I didn't even respond. I just got my shit back on and dropped a few hundred on the table because I knew it would make her mad.

When I came out the room, Khalid was standing in the hallway with his bedroom door open. I didn't even bother to acknowledge him. I just pulled my fitted cap down on my head further and went about my business. I needed to make this paper before the block got hot, and Street better had handled that shit by the time I got back around there.

Joey Street

Life in the Fast Lane

I deaded that nigga. I just closed my eyes and pulled the trigger. What choice did I have? It was either kill or be killed, and even though he was my girl's blood, what could I do? He violated the code of the streets, and since I wasn't ready to meet my maker, I had to make moves. They wanted me to ditch the body as well, and that wasn't a problem, because I was good at covering my tracks, but looking Shanyce in the face would prove to be difficult, knowing what I did. The good thing was that his family was used to him being gone for days, so they wouldn't suspect anything at first. The funeral would be the bullshit, and mentally, I wasn't ready for none of it.

His body slid to the side and hit the floor in slow motion, taking the chair with him, and I was speechless. The silencer on the gun made a world of difference, but the shit felt hot in my hands, and my reflexes caused me to drop the gun at my feet. Bird and Choice had satisfied looks on their faces, and I supposed that was a good thing, since I was the one that was still standing.

I went into autopilot, cutting the rope from the tilted chair that he was tied to and moving the chair out of the way so that I could stretch his body out on the carpet. I rolled his ass up like I was rolling a long-ass Dutch, and tucked him tightly in the corner until I could make that move. I didn't even bother to look at Choice and Bird. Instead, I went into the bathroom to wash my face and to check my clothes for blood. I knew they wouldn't let me go home to change if my clothes were a mess.

Despite a few droplets of blood on the toe of my Tims, I was still in business. I used a paper towel to wet the spot and try to dab it off, but that proved to be useless, so I shook that shit off, because I couldn't do anything about it now. I went into the living room to watch TV, where Choice and Bird were now sitting.

I wanted to call Shanyce, but I knew if I even thought about reaching for my phone, it would be a problem. They left my phone right there to tempt me, but it must have been turned off because it wasn't vibrating or anything. I knew Shanyce had to have called me at the very least a thousand times, but I had to play it cool. Once I ditched the body, I could go home.

My mouth felt like cotton, and I was suddenly hungry as shit. These dudes were watching my every move to see how I would react or if I would spaz out, but I played it cool. I just took my bag of food from the table and popped the shit in the microwave so that I could get my grub on. I didn't even bother to ask for the cup of orange juice I took from his refrigerator, since I had left mine in my ride. Although I knew Choice didn't allow eating in his living room, I took my shit right back in there and ate it.

He didn't say a word; his look said it all. I acted like I ain't even see that shit as I enjoyed my breakfast platter from earlier and watched TV.

"We gonna move the body out around ten when the block dies down. We'll take it out the back way and move towards the park," I said to them after I was done eating and my stomach felt satisfied. I figured we had a better chance of moving the body out the back door, just in case some fiends were out, or the law was driving by.

Choice shook his head in acknowledgment and Bird continued to look at me like he was dissecting me or something. Fuck that nigga. I had other shit on my mind, like how the hell I was gonna get out the game and move my family away from this bullshit. I didn't want my son thinking this shit was his only option, because even though we never talked about it, I knew he was aware of what I did. He stayed too fly to be getting that shit off of a working man's salary, and he always had the newest shit out.

I sat back in Choice's plush-ass chair and allowed my eyes to close for what felt like a brief second. I was instantly taken back to that day down the park when I was twelve years old. There were these two guys I used to roll with, Adam and Gabriel, that lived out Bartram Village. We would always go sit by this huge wall that the Schuylkill River ran next to. Across the park they had an entire play set, complete with a slide and jungle gym, but we felt like we were way too smooth for that and opted to converse by the rock wall and talk about our week.

On the low, Gabriel always hated Adam because Adam's mom kept him in Stacey Adams, khaki pants, and Polo shirts. He didn't run around the Ville in dusty jeans and hand-me-down T-shirts like Gabriel did, and although I wasn't stepping out in Staceys, mom dukes kept me on point in the latest gear, and I stayed with a fresh cut.

On this particular day, I was rocking this fresh to death light blue Adidas sweat suit with the white strips down the side of the legs and the big Adidas emblem on the back of my jacket. I had on a pure white Kangol hat and a white wife beater underneath that had me thinking I was looking like LL Cool J in his "Rock the Bells" video. My mom promised me a herringbone chain for my birthday just like the one LL had, and I couldn't wait.

We were sitting by the wall debating about who had the better power out of the Fantastic Four when Gabriel heard a noise on the other side of the wall.

"Y'all hear that?" he asked with this strange look on his face. We got quiet and listened, and it surely sounded like something was trying to climb up the wall. Now, we knew there were abandoned cars and shit that were in the water, and it wasn't uncommon to see a body floating up the river either.

Chancing a look on the other side, we breathed a sigh of relief when all we saw were live crabs clawing at the wall. I couldn't believe it myself, because as dirty and dark brown as that water was, how could anything survive in it?

"Yo, I dare you to grab one of them crabs out the water," Gabriel said to Adam as we watched the crabs fight each other to stay on top.

A part of me thinks that beside the fact that Adam stayed fly, the reason why Gabriel picked on him so much was because out of all of us, he was the shortest and he wasn't really a fighter. Adam was too busy trying to stay clean to get into a scuffle. He was also an only child, so unlike most of the other kids that lived in the projects, he didn't have any brothers or sisters to back him up in a tussle, so he tried to stay cool with everyone.

"You know that water is too low for him to grab those things," I said to Gabriel's hating-ass self, taking a look at him for a brief second.

"Naw, he can reach them. I'll hold his legs," Gabriel insisted.

"What is you tryin'a do? Catch dinner, man?" Adam joked, not realizing that was a bad move.

Shit got tense real fast, so I had to say something to keep it from being a damn fight. The thing is, I liked Adam just as much as I liked Gabriel, and I didn't want to have to choose between the two of them.

"Whatever, nigga, just come on. And tell your mom I want some extra Old Bay on them shits when she done cooking them," Gabriel said, positioning himself by the wall to hold Adam over.

"Yo, nigga, he can't reach them shits. I don't want no parts of it," I said, jumping back from the wall. From what I saw, there was an abandoned car down there and some other nasty shit, but Gabriel was just trying to be a smart ass. Adam was too scared not to do it, so I walked back and stood next to the tree to watch these two idiots try to get some dusty-ass crabs from out the water.

Leaning against the tree, all I could think about was how mad Adam's mom was going to be when she saw how dirty his clothes would get from hanging over that wall. I could not believe his simple ass was going through with that shit, but Adam would have to learn to man up one of these days. It looked like it was going smooth at first, but after a while, Gabriel started looking like he was losing his grip. Adam was head first over the wall, and he was screaming for Gabriel to pull him back up. He couldn't get a grip on the wall or the crabs, because the moss made it slippery.

It felt like I was moving in slow motion as I ran over there to try to help, and just as I approached them, Adam's feet slipped through Gabriel's arms and he went face first into the water.

"What are you doing?" I screamed at Gabriel as I looked on the other side.

Adam was still lying face down in the water, and a dark cloud of red started to form around his head as he floated on the water. The tide looked like it was threatening to push his body downstream, but it appeared that his shirt collar must have gotten caught on the abandoned car, keeping his body where it was. Gabriel stood frozen with a scared look on his face, and I'm sure my fear matched his as well.

"Gabriel, go get help! Go get help!" I screamed at him while I kept an eye on Adam's body, making sure it stayed put. Gabriel stood frozen for a moment longer before he turned and ran at top speed up Gypsy Hill, the name we gave to Fifty-sixth Street because of the steep hill that led to Bartram's Garden.

It felt like an eternity, and by the time Adam's mom made it downhill, I knew it was too late. Adam was dead. The blood never stopped flowing, and the water just got redder as some of the other adults that came down to be nosey tried to keep Adam's mom from jumping in to save her boy. Shortly after, we could hear police sirens approaching. I couldn't stop crying as I was held by my own mother, who appeared out of nowhere.

There were so many cops and news people by the water that we all had to step back to give them room. When they pulled Adam's body from the water, his eyes were closed and he had a smile on his face.

"Yo, nigga, wake ya ass up. It's time to make moves," Choice said, nudging my foot as he walked by. I sat up in the chair and wiped my forehead, not believing the amount of sweat that covered my face. I'd been having that nightmare for years, and I couldn't believe I let myself get so comfortable as to fall into a dead sleep in front of these niggas.

I jumped up out of my seat and disposed of my trash before I grabbed my cell phone from the table and moved toward the room. It took only two of us to carry the body out, and we made sure we wore gloves so that there wouldn't be any fingerprints. We placed the body in the trunk and moved down toward Bartram's Garden. I'd ditched so many dead bodies down there, but never in the water. Adam's memory wouldn't allow me to do it, and when Gabriel was murdered down there and strung up on a tree five short years later, I felt no sorrow, because he took his last breaths where Adam took his. It was all Gabriel's fault, and even though I never snitched on him, I never trusted him again either.

We drove deep into the woods with only flashlights on either side of the window because headlights would be too bright. Bird and I got him out of the carpet and propped his body up against a tree, where someone would find him stinking days from now. I took the gloves from my hands and Bird's, and after dropping him and Choice off on the block, I disposed of that shit in the incinerator in the Forty-sixth Street projects. I took the gun to a friend of mine that worked at a steel mill. He would melt the gun down like he'd done for me in the past, and there would no traces of it ever.

Driving back down the way, I parked the whip in front of Choice's crib, where I still saw Vince's shit parked, and I got into my own Jeep so that I could take it back on the block. It was one in the morning at this point, and I didn't even bother to go into the room with Shanyce. Instead, after kissing my son on the forehead, I stretched out on the couch and lay there in the dark, too afraid to close my eyes this soon.

I could live with the nightmares, but it was the dirt I did that caused them and in reality, I didn't have too many choices. Once you commit one crime, you're a criminal for life. This was the life I chose; it didn't choose me. My only goal was to make it better for my son.

Journey Clayton

Snow Day

I didn't see Khalid for almost a week after that night because the next day, we were hit with a damn snowstorm that shut the city down for a week. For a child, that's normally a good thing, because instead of sitting in school all day, we could be outside playing in the snow and making snowmen. Once I found out that Khalid was on punishment, that took a lot of the fun out of it, but when Vince told me that since I didn't have school I would be spending my time cooking and bagging up product, that killed it for me.

I didn't even bother to go to the window when I heard other children outside playing, and when the healthcare worker called and said that she couldn't come until later that night, I knew this was going to be a dumb-ass week.

Despite the snow, Vince's ass still showed the hell up, though, and just looking at him made me sick to my stomach.

While he was in the room, I was in the kitchen washing dishes, but I knew he was up to something. Leaving the water running and taking my shoes off, I tiptoed over to the room to see what he was doing. Just as I suspected, he moved the picture my mom had of black Jesus from off the wall and pulled a latch that revealed a hole that had money and product stuffed in it. He wasn't even smart enough to have a lock on it.

I went back to the sink and continued washing the dishes, afterward setting the table so that I could start cooking things up.

Vince sat in the living room and switched between watching me and watching the TV. I felt like I was under a magnifying glass as I cooked up mounds of the white powder that the streets called Snow White. I thought about Khalid briefly, but I thought more about the stuff that Vince had in the wall. It was weird that both he and Joey decided to hide their stuff in a room with their loved ones, but Vince didn't exactly love me, so I guess that's how it was going to be. He did what he felt he had to do.

He allowed me only two bathroom breaks, and around four, he walked me over to Bartram Village so that Ms. Toya could braid my hair again. This was only my second trip to her house, but I was already looking forward to my visit. Her phone conversation had me in stitches the last time I was there, and I was looking forward to hearing her cursing somebody out. I had some questions that I needed answered myself; I just had to find a way to slide them in there like it wasn't me I was talking about.

She was standing outside waiting when we walked up, and I came to the conclusion that her and my uncle Vince were still going at it, because she just snatched the money out of his hands and walked into the building, not even bothering to speak or anything like that. I didn't even know I was coming today, because had I known, I would have at least started taking my hair out. I wasn't mad, though, because that just meant I would be there longer.

I looked for Ms. Reid when I got inside, but she wasn't there. I didn't know if they shared a place or what, because it was a two-bedroom unit, but since it wasn't my business, I didn't ask.

"Journey, your hair held up good," Toya said to me as she unraveled my braids with a metal-tip rat-tail comb. It still looked cute because it was all crinkly when she unraveled it, but once she pulled that wide-tooth comb through it, I was back to having a wild bush.

I climbed up on the drain board like before and covered my eyes with the towel so that she could wash and scrub my hair. I had my eyes closed and under the towel, so I didn't realize that she had taken her shirt off until I lifted up to get down from the sink. My eyes popped wide open as I took in her curves and the small butterfly tattoo that sat to the left of her belly button on her flat stomach.

Her breasts sat up perfectly in her navy blue and orange cream bra, and on the way back down, I could see the rim of her panties because her jeans were unbuttoned. When she turned around, I noticed she had on a thong again, and I knew I had to ask some questions before I rolled out. If I didn't have anything else when I grew up, I had to have a body like hers.

"So, what you been up to since the last time you was here?" Toya asked as she parted my hair into sections to dry it.

"The same ol' stuff. Going to school and studying with Khalid. He really liked my hair," I said, blushing a little as I remembered the look on Khalid's face when I walked up the morning after I got my hair done.

"Ohhh, so you have a boyfriend?" Toya said in a singsong voice that made me giggle and blush even more.

"Well, he's not exactly my boyfriend, but we do spend a lot of time together," I said to her shyly. I wanted to ask her so many things, but where should I start?

"Khalid . . ." Toya said as if she was trying to place a face with the name. "That's Street's son, right?"

"Mr. Joey, you mean?" I ask to make sure we were talking about the same person. I knew Khalid's last name was Street, but I didn't know that they called his dad by it.

"Yeah, that's him. Khalid is a handsome little boy. Y'all kissed yet?" she asked on the sly that made me blush again. I didn't want her to think I was loose and that we were already having relations, but Khalid kissed me all the time, so I assumed he liked me.

"Once or twice," I responded shyly, giggling.

"Let me tell you something about boys, Journey," she said to me as she continued to part my hair into big sections to prepare me for blow-drying.

"A kiss don't mean shit. You're too young right now to understand it, and it's not to say that Khalid doesn't like you, but a boy will kiss you just to trick you into thinking he likes you so he can get your goodies. You're not having sex yet, are you?"

"No! I never thought about it," I responded, surprised by her mode of questioning. I knew I was about to learn a serious life lesson, so I paid close attention to what she would say next.

"I had to ask. Shit, I been fuckin' since I was like ten years old. True story. And I made some mistakes along the way, but understand that giving everybody your pussy won't leave you with anything but a wet ass and dry pockets. You're too young right now, but if you stick around long enough, I'll school you on what's really good, so that you won't get caught out there."

"Wow. I'm not anywhere near out there, and besides Khalid, I don't talk to any other boys."

"That's cool, but what has Khalid given you for those kisses?" she asked before pulling the blow dryer comb through my damp hair. My hair was thick and nappy at the root, so I had to brace myself, since Toya was not gentle when she did my hair. I didn't want to have to talk over the dryer, so I waited until she was done to answer.

"He lets me wear his chain while we're in school," I finally responded to her question. It made me feel real special, because I knew Gina got jealous that she wasn't the one with it on.

"That doesn't mean shit," she said, crushing all of my hopes and dreams. "That just means he's marking his territory so that no one else will step to you."

"Well, why would anyone else want me? No one else has said anything to me before." I was completely puzzled now. Khalid and I shared so much, yet so little, because I was so embarrassed by my situation. I did wonder every so often what made him just approach me after all this time. We spent four grades in the same class and he never stepped to me before.

"That's the thing. He saw something in you that maybe the other boys in your class hadn't yet, and he stepped to you before anyone else saw it." She said while combing my hair roughly.

"He lets you wear his chain at school, huh? And that means what to you? See if he'll let you wear it overnight, and then you'll know what's really good."

I sat there and took it all in, and for the very first time, I had doubts about where me and Khalid's relationship was going. He was so attentive and carried my books and everything. He never allowed anyone to say anything sideways to me, even though I was sure they did on the low, but Khalid was like my savior, and it was safe to say that I almost loved him for that. So why would he try to play me?

"So, is that why you wear thongs all the time? To keep your boyfriend from looking at other girls?" I asked innocently. I wanted a thong; I just doubted that Vince would let me have them.

"Girl," Toya burst out, laughing almost to the point where I thought she was going to fall out of the chair. "I wear thongs because bloomers are for old people. I'm only twenty-one, and my ass is like *whoa* in these jeans. I'm not about to let a panty line ruin it."

I laughed along with her as she continued to break down how boys work and how I had to always stay a step ahead so that a boy couldn't play me. She told me that if I wasn't gaining anything from giving a boy my goodies, then I needed to keep my goodies to myself.

Suddenly, I knew that's exactly how I would have to be with my uncle Vince from now on. I was tired of performing oral sex for him just for the benefit of my mother; it was time I came up on this deal as well. I needed a new coat, and by the end of the week, I planned to have one.

I was definitely learning from Toya, and I knew she would be the one to help me out. I was confused about so many things, like why my uncle treated me the way he did, and what I felt for Khalid. I didn't know if I would ever tell anyone my secret, but I knew I would eventually develop a plan to better deal with it.

Vincent Clayton

Soldier Boy

Once again, it took forever for Toya to do my niece's hair, because I know bitches just can't sit down to get they hair done, they gotta gossip the entire time. I was pissed because I was out here in the damn snow, still hustling. Fiends don't give a damn about no snowfall; they trudge right through that shit to get what they need. Who am I to deny them satisfaction? I really didn't mind the cold, but this shit was undrivable, so I had to walk every-gotdamn-where, which took extra long when you had snow up to your ass, and I wasn't in the mood.

I could have gone home like three in the morning when the snow first started to fall, but I didn't think it would be that bad, and I didn't want to chance getting stuck out in Bala Cynwood if the snow got to be too deep. My dogs were in the crib, so I wasn't worried about that either; I just hoped they didn't tear up my shit too much before I got back.

That was four days ago, and I was getting more aggravated by the day, so I was trying to keep my cool.

In the four days that Journey had been out of school, she cooked up enough product to last us a couple of weeks, depending on the flow of business. As a reward, I took her to get her hair done, to teach her that if she wanted to keep getting her hair done and getting nice clothes, she would have to put in work. Nothing in this world came for free, and if I did nothing else, I would drill this in her head, even if it killed me. Shit, the only reason why she wasn't on the block was because she was a girl. Let her had been my nephew instead, and he'd be right the fuck out here in the trenches, hustling like the rest of us. If Street was smart, his boy would have been on the block already, too, but I guess everyone has their values.

When I went to pick up Journey, there was something different about her. I couldn't quite put my finger on it, but something in her had changed. On the way over, she was barely making it through the snow and I had to help her up like a thousand times. On the way back, she flowed through like that shit was easy, and I was the one stumbling all over the place.

"Journey, when you get upstairs, I left a small batch on the table for you to finish up. Have it done by the time I get back," I said to her when we got in front of the door.

She didn't even reply. She just turned and sashayed her ass up the steps and let herself in. I noticed her little ass bouncing around in her sweatpants, and my dick got hard instantly. I knew Journey was going to have a hell of a shape when she got older, and if nothing else, I would be the first to tap that shit.

Turning to adjust my dick in my boxers, I contemplated at least getting some head before I rolled out, but I kept it moving. She had a lot of making up to do, and I would collect when time permitted.

I served a few fiends on my way down to Choice's crib.

Him and Bird was sitting on the stoop when I walked by, and he had some information on Bunz that we needed to talk about, because I was ready to put the nigga to rest as well. I thought for sure when he got knocked last week that he would be in there singing like a canary, but he got out on some bullshit restitution because the owner of the restaurant picked the wrong guy out of the lineup. We needed to do damage control, though, because it wouldn't be long before his simple ass slipped up and mentioned Street's name in that bullshit-ass robbery, and we needed to dead that nigga before then.

"Yo, it's gonna be a minute before they find that nigga. It must be at least ten feet of snow out this bitch, and you know ain't nobody going anywhere near the damn park for a while," Choice said to Bird as I was walking up, referring to Shanyce's deceased brother. Joey ditched the body a couple days ago, but since it snowed, we hadn't seen him. I guess he felt bad, but he'd be cool. You stop giving a fuck once you get enough bodies on you.

"They'll find him in the spring once the snow melts," Bird said, laughing. "They talking about another storm hitting in like two more days. The city gonna be shut down for a while."

"That's why we need to get at Bunz now. I just saw his scab ass sitting on the stoop out the Ville when I went to get my niece from Toya's," I said as I walked up the steps and leaned against the door. Bird passed me the L they were puffing on and we continued the rotation and our conversation, discussing what needed to go down. I wanted to take him out then, but I didn't want to cause a scene, and 5-o had been out heavy all day.

"I say we should let Street dead that nigga. He the one got Street in this shit in the first place,"

Choice suggested. I was feeling him on that shit, too, because if nothing else,

Street needed to learn how to work that revenge thing if he was going to stick around. Leave no witnesses standing.

"You tryin'a make that nigga a full man overnight, huh?" I laughed at Bird as we continued to pass the Dutch around. Bird was the regulator. He was the one that picked and trained new soldiers that came on, and I think a part of him felt like he failed a little when it came to Street.

"Not overnight, but we definitely about to speed up the process. Where that nigga at anyway? I ain't seen him since the snow hit," Bird said, choking on blunt smoke. I swear he choked damn near every time because he inhaled so deep. "He had some shit to handle with his seed, and you know he ain't thuggin' it out in the snow. Shanyce got that ass on lock," I replied, remembering the blessing I got from her ass just days earlier. I swear she had the strongest jaws in Southwest Philly.

"I need to see her about some shit. It's been a minute since I been hypnotized," Choice said, causing me to laugh. I knew exactly what he meant, because Shanyce's ass swayed side to side while she sucked your dick, like she was a snake charmer. She would have you stuck on stupid if you wasn't careful. That would be a quick nut for sure.

"Dude, definitely get up in that. I was over there the other day, and everything is still on point."

Choice and Bird burst into laughter because they knew how I got down. Since they had Street occupied, I went and slipped on over there. I just wasn't banking on his boy seeing me leave, but I wasn't worried about it. That was for Shanyce to handle. Everybody who was anybody knew his mom was a whore. I guess now he knew too.

"So, what we gonna do about Bunz simple ass? I'm ready to walk to the Ville now and off that nigga," Bird said with mad irritation in his voice.

Dead people can't testify. He lived by that shit day in and day out, and would off anyone that could possibly infiltrate our business. Nobody was getting it like us around here, and if a threat occurred, we handled that shit immediately. Street snuck one in on us, and we knew making that nigga murder would really fuck his head up. We hoped to make him immune to feeling bad afterward, too, and for Joey, it had to happen soon. We didn't just let you out of the game, and if he continued to prove himself to be useless, Shanyce would be getting that good black dress popping sooner than she wanted to.

"Naw, Bunz will get his in due time. I'ma walk around the spot and see what Street getting into. Maybe I can convince him to come make some money," I said with a laugh. I hadn't met a nigga yet that I had to convince to make some change, but Street seemed to be a different breed. I gave my boys some dap, and started around the corner to see what Street was up too, promising them that I wouldn't be gone too long.

In the five or six feet of snow that blanketed the pavement, the three-minute walk turned into a ten-minute struggle as I dipped and dived around mountains of snow until I got onto Street's block. From the corner, I could see him out shoveling a path from his door to his neighbor's. They said there was more snow coming, so shoveling now would be useless, but I guess if he cleaned up some now, it wouldn't be as much later on.

He was really into what he was doing, and didn't feel me up on him until the last minute. I could see his boy in the upstairs window looking out, but when he noticed me looking back, he backed away from the window and closed the curtain. I guess the little nigga was still upset about the other day.

"What's up, Street? We ain't seen you in a while," I said as I knocked a little of the snow back onto the now cleaned space. He looked at

me like he was annoyed, then shoveled the snow
back up and continued to make a path.

"Yo, wassup, Vince? This snow got a brother
on lock, but I was gonna get at y'all," he said unconvincingly.

"I feel you. I just came to check on you. We
wanted to talk to you about your position, but
I see you're a little busy, so . . ." I started backing up from the sidewalk so that he could finish
shoveling.

He looked up at me as if to register what I just
said, and I gave him a look that hopefully told
him I was serious.

"Okay, well, just let me get my situation with
my family in order and I'll stop past later," he
said just as Shanyce opened the door. We both
stopped and looked at her, and I had to keep my
mouth from falling open. Why in hell she would
come to the door in a sheer robe and nothing
underneath is beyond me. A small part of me
thought she wanted Street to know she was a
"scunt." That's what we called chicks that we
considered skanks and cunts, and Shanyce definitely fit the bill. I could see her dark nipples and
her hairless pussy through the flimsy robe, and
my dick instantly jumped to attention.

"Joey, I need you upstairs. I can't reach some
stuff in the top of the closet," she said without

looking my way. I knew enough to know that her pussy was pulsating and she probably wanted both our asses at the same time.

"Street, I'll see you later, man," I said to him, not even bothering to wait for a response.

As I walked away, I could hear him cursing her out about coming to the door half naked, and when I looked back, I could see their son in the window looking at me again. It looked like he held up his hands as if he was holding a gun and shooting at me, but it could have just been my imagination.

I turned and kept it moving so that I could get back to Choice's crib. I really wanted to be sitting gripped in some tight pussy, but a player can't have it all—or can he? I thought briefly about doubling back to the projects and digging Toya's back out, but no one wanted pussy with attitude attached to it, so I decided against it. I would be keeping my eye on Khalid, though, because if I had to get his little ass laid down, it could happen. I would talk to Joey about it at a later date. Right now, we had business to handle.

Joey Street

If the Price is Right

"Yo, what the fuck made you come to the door like that? You want everybody seeing what my pussy look like?"

I swear Shanyce did the dumbest shit all the damn time. For the life of me, I couldn't figure out what I saw in her simple ass, besides the fact that she was a snake charmer, but I was really starting to feel like that wasn't enough to keep her around. My heart wouldn't let me walk out on Khalid, either, but eventually I wouldn't have a choice. He'd just have to understand.

"Joey, please. Ain't nobody thinking about me. Vince didn't even look my way," she said as she turned to walk up the steps.

"So, you knew he was out there and you came to the door like that anyway? What day he gets to fuck you on? Wednesdays?" I asked, remembering how the guy at the breakfast spot came at me.

Trying to turn a ho into a housewife was proving
to be a bit more than I could stand.

"Here we go with this shit again," she said as
she continued up the steps and into our room.

I closed the bedroom door once I caught up
with her, so that Khalid wouldn't hear us arguing, and I lowered my voice, hoping she would
follow suit. I was really fucking pissed. I mean, I
heard shit all the time about our bedroom having
a revolving door, but I tried to pay it no mind.
Was it true, though? Was Shanyce really out
there acting a fool right under my damn nose?

"What the fuck did you have to get that couldn't
wait until I was done shoveling, Shanyce?" I asked
her as I backed her into a corner. I was ready to
put her head through the damn wall, and I swear I
think she liked getting hit on. Some women don't
feel loved unless you're knocking them in the
fucking head and shit.

"I just wanted my pumps from the top of the
closet."

"And you were going to wear them where?
Outside in six feet of fuckin' snow dressed in lingerie? You a simple bitch, I swear," I said, turning away from her to leave the house. Every time
I thought we could get back on track, we were
right back at square one. The only reason why I
was still there was for my son, but I felt more and

more that I'd be having that talk with him about how shit was gonna be.

"I know you don't think you leaving," she said, trying to grab my arm. Before I knew it, I turned around and gripped her up, slamming her body against the wall. I wanted to put her lights out on some real shit, but I couldn't see deadin' her ass and having to explain it to my son.

"Shanyce, I'm leaving this house and I'll be back later. When I get back, you better have a different attitude, or it's going to be a problem. Understand?"

She looked like she was too scared to even speak, and opted to shake her head yes instead of voicing her answer. I didn't even realize that her feet weren't touching the floor until I let her go and she landed in a heap in the corner. I grabbed my hat off a dresser and rolled out of the house, checking to make sure my boy was cool before bouncing out. I took the time to finish shoveling the path I had started before putting the shovel back in the door and walking around the corner. I was surprised that Shanyce didn't come back to the door to try to finish the argument.

I went right up to Choice's spot because I knew that's where they would be when they weren't outside. I could hear a basketball game playing on the TV from the hallway, and I figured they must have been watching ESPN.

Everyone greeted me when I walked in. I passed on the rotation because I needed to have a level head when dealing with these guys. In all honesty, I was still fucked up about grounding Shanyce's brother, and as the days went by, I got more tense waiting for them to find the body.

The snowfall made that much more difficult, because we got hit with like six feet, and another storm was coming, so I knew it would be a while before they found him. They probably wouldn't be able to physically identify his body because it was sure to be decomposed by then. I made sure to take chunks out of his face, and damaged all tattoos that could be easily identified. Choice and Bird just stood back and watched me in amazement as I worked. I had to cover my tracks; it was as simple as that.

"Joey Street, what it do, nigga?" Vince asked, giving me dap. They were all high as kites up in this joint, and I was hoping that I hadn't made a mistake coming by this early. Maybe I should have waited a day.

"You know me. Gettin' in where I fit in," I replied as I made myself semi-comfortable on the couch. I didn't plan to stay long, so I hoped they would just get right to the point of having me here.

"What's up with that Bunz situation? You handle that nigga yet?" Bird asked me as he was just receiving the blunt they were passing around.

"Naw. I haven't really seen him since on the news a while ago. Why you ask?"

"Because he a nut-ass stick-up kid that may become a potential problem. He got a price on his head now," Choice said to me, although he never took his eyes from the television screen.

"And what's the price?" I asked, trying to appear like I wasn't shook. I was guessing that they were trying to make me a real hit man overnight, because although I ran product for them, I was always the one ditching bodies and on occasions taking people out. The real question was did I have it in me to maintain that kind of persona? Was I a killer for real? I mean, I laid plenty of people to rest, but was that really how I got down?

"On the real, this one should be a freebie, since you did that nut-ass robbery with him, but just to make it fair I'll toss ten thousand on his head. I figured he's worth a dime if nothing else," Choice said, finally turning to me.

I had to think about it, because on some real shit, I should have pumped lead into that nigga that night, but I let him walk. I had a feeling that eventually some shit was going to go wrong and

I would have to dead him anyway, but since he
had a price now, I might as well take it.

"How much time do I have?" I asked, trying
to calculate what I needed to do. It wouldn't
be a problem getting that nigga by himself, but
he was always carrying, so I had to make sure I
wasn't the one that got dropped in the process.

"We'll get him here for you, so don't sweat it.
Just be ready when the time comes," Bird said
as he tried to pass me the L for the fourth time.
I took it and handed that shit right to Vince. I
needed to keep a level head, and since this was
the only option they were giving me to prove myself, I had to take advantage until I was able to jet
out of here for good.

I left the crib and made my way to the corner
store, since they opened up whether it was snow
to the ceiling or not, and got me and my boy a
couple of hoagies to eat for a late lunch. I knew
he saw and heard things that he shouldn't have,
so I would have to sit him down and talk to him
eventually. I thought briefly about getting Shanyce something, but I was still pissed at her
simple ass, so she would have to defrost something if her ass was hungry. Fuck her.

When I got back to the crib, Shanyce was sitting on the couch with the shades drawn and
candles lit, looking like she had been crying for

the last half hour. She was now dressed in sweat-pants and a wife beater, and her hair was pulled back in a ponytail. I walked right past her ass like I didn't see her lying there, and she started crying louder as I walked up the steps. I kept the shit moving all the way to my son's room, where he was inside playing his Nintendo 64.

"Hey, wassup, li'l man? I got something for you to eat," I said to him, pulling out his turkey and cheese sandwich, chips, and juice. He didn't even bother to turn around; he just continued to play his game as if I wasn't there.

"Khalid, you not hungry, man?" I asked him, sensing something was wrong.

"Was you and Mommy arguing about Uncle Vince?" he asked, pausing his game and finally turning to face me. "Why you ask that?"

"Because y'all always arguing about him. He made her cry the other day."

I was floored for like ten whole seconds before I was able to respond. What was he talking about? I hadn't seen Vince around here since the day before we handled Shanyce's brother, and she never mentioned him coming here, so where the hell was I? More importantly, what were they arguing about?

"Why was she crying?" I asked him, not sure if I even wanted to know why.

"I don't know. She was mad at me, and you wouldn't answer your phone. Then Vince showed up, and they were arguing in the room. It sounded like she was crying."

"In what room? The living room?" I asked him so that I could be sure of what he was trying to tell me. For Shanyce's sake, he had better say they were downstairs.

"No, they were in the bedroom for a while. I saw Vince leave, and Mommy got up and slammed the door shut."

I had to pace back and forth for a second to get my head on straight, because it was about to go down. Did she fuck that nigga while my son was here? I might have another body under my belt sooner than I thought, because if she didn't answer my questions right, it would be over for her ass tonight.

"Listen, put your boots and stuff on. I'm going to see if you can chill with Journey for a while so I can talk to your mom," I said while I dialed Vince's number.

Once I explained to him what was really good, he agreed to meet me on the corner so that he could walk Khalid to his niece's house. I promised him that he wouldn't have to be there for too long; I just had to straighten some things out at home. Vince agreed, so I gathered all of

Khalid's food back into the bag with the things I had bought for myself, so that he and Journey could have lunch, and we made our way down the steps.

"Where are you taking my son?" Shanyce yelled at me as we came down the steps. I tried to ignore her, but she was making shit difficult.

"I'm going to Journey's house, Mom. Uncle Vince said it was okay," Khalid answered as we walked toward the door.

Shanyce looked like she wanted to object, but the look I gave her shut her right up. I took a few seconds to walk my boy to meet Vince at the corner, and watched them until he got into Journey's house before I turned back around. I would holla at Vince later on, too, depending on how this conversation with Shanyce went. As for right now, Shanyce better be on point, or she would be getting fucked up before the day was out, guaranteed.

Journey Clayton

Pinky Swear

When my uncle called and told me that Khalid was on his way around to chill with me, I
couldn't believe it. Vince never let me have com-
pany, because he didn't want people to know
about my mom, but I wasn't about to question
him on why he changed his mind today. I made
sure everything was in place, and I pulled out
some microwave popcorn so that we could watch
a movie. I was so excited about seeing Khalid,
because I hadn't seen him since before the snowstorm began, when he got in trouble.

When he got there, he seemed a little upset
about something, but I didn't want to question
him in front of my uncle. I graciously took the
food that he offered from the corner store, and
somewhat rushed Vince out of the house so that
we could finally catch up.

"Khalid, I am so happy to see you," I said to him with a wide smile on my face while we embraced. He hugged me back just as tight, and then we sat down to eat and catch up. "I'm going to kill your uncle one of these days," he said to me between bites of his food.

I had to pause and look at him, not believing my ears. He looked beyond pissed. I had never seen him like this before. "Why you say that?" I asked him, curious as to what brought on these thoughts. I had yet to confide in him about what was going on with me and Vince and my mother's situation, so something else must have gone down to cause his ill feelings toward my uncle. Not that I was opposed to Vince being killed, but I still had things to get from him, and I wasn't ready for him to die just yet. I hated Vince more than anyone, because I couldn't understand why he treated me like he did. Him being murdered wouldn't be all that bad, but then I would be forced into foster care. I was torn between wanting him gone and maybe just dealing with the shit to stay free.

"He's sleeping with my mom behind my dad's back, and my mom acts like I don't know what's going on."

Once again, I was left speechless. Khalid went ahead and told me about Vince's visit over there the other day, and although he didn't see the actual sexual act, he heard it, and when Vince left, he was standing in the hallway. He was mad because his mom made him go back into his room and threatened to beat his ass if he told his father Vince was there. Apparently this had been going on for a while, because from what Khalid told me, Vince wasn't the only one from the crew that visited his mother's bedroom.

"Say it ain't so, Khalid," was my only response. I couldn't believe everything he just told me. "Oh, it's so. My mom's a ho."

I felt bad for Khalid. I had no idea his mom got down like that, and I knew if that shit got out, it would be over for him at school. I was worse off, though. My mom was a junkie dying from AIDS, and I had to keep that secret bottled up in me so that no one would find out. Something told me I could trust Khalid, though, and I tossed the idea back and forth about whether I should tell him. We were in similar situations, and I figured maybe we could help each other through these tough times. We honestly didn't have anyone else we could depend on.

"Your secret is safe with me, Khalid. I won't tell anyone," I said to him, holding out my pinky so that he could connect his with mine.

"Pinky swear?" he said to me upon connection.

"Pinky swear," I said back to him before we continued to eat our food.

I thought briefly about the stuff Toya told me about boys, and I decided that Khalid was trustworthy. After all, I was going to be his wife one day, so I didn't want to have any secrets between us. He had just dropped some heavy shit on me about his mom, but what I was going to show him was way over the top, and I wasn't sure if he could handle it.

"I don't want any secrets between us, Khalid. I want us to always be best friends," I said to him as I tried to find a way to share my most intimate secret with him. Well, not the most, because I still didn't have the heart to tell him about me and Vince's agreement, but my mom was just as heavy a secret as any.

"Forever and ever," he said to me and we embraced again.

"Okay, there's something I need to show you. I just need to know that you'll ride with me through anything."

Instead of responding, he took the last bite of his sandwich into his mouth and stood up, grabbing my hand, so that I could show him my big secret. Taking a look at the clock again, I saw that it was time to give my mom her next shot, and I couldn't procrastinate any longer. If I didn't give my mom her shots on time, she started to shake uncontrollably, and that only made it harder for me to find a vein. I didn't want to show him all the gruesome details right away, but I decided I might as well get it over with.

I took a few minutes to gather everything I needed, and I ushered him into my mother's bedroom so that he could see what was really going on around here. He seemed afraid and opted to stand by the door. I went on and took care of my business like he was not even there.

I was talking to my mom in the process, introducing her to Khalid and just having a general one-sided conversation, because she had the glazed look. By the time I was finished cooking up her fix and injecting it, she was already in a nod. Khalid looked like he was ready to jet up out of there, and for the first time, I thought just maybe I showed him a little too much too soon. Him having a ho for a mom is one thing, and his dad being a drug dealer is something else, but for him to see drug use and the effects of it up close and personal could be a bit much for the average child to take in. I hadn't been average in over a year.

I had mixed emotions now that I'd opened myself up to him. How would I cope if he rolled

out on me? When I said I had no one to turn
to, I was dead serious. I was isolated from my
mother's family years ago when she first started
showing signs of being strung out, and my dad's
family never liked my mom, so they stayed clear
as well. The only person that ever stepped in
was Vince, and he had his own wicked reasons
why he came through, so I was left ass out completely. Khalid was like a light in the darkness
that surrounded my very being, and now it was
possible that I might be back in the dark again.
He stayed glued to the door jamb while I cleaned
up, and shortly after I tucked my mom in, he left
the room. I walked into the living room with my
head down, not sure what I should say at this
point. That was the real, no chaser, and either he
was going to stick around for it, or he was going
to jet. I liked Khalid a lot, but if I had to choose,
it would be my mom. She was all I had for the
time being.

He had this strange look on his face that I
couldn't read. I didn't know if my showing him
how I was really living was a good idea, but it
would come out eventually, so what choice did
I have? This was me, the real me, and he was
either going to accept it or he wasn't.

He was sitting on the couch by the door, looking like he was contemplating staying or going.

Back stiff, hands in his lap, and a blank look on his face was all the emotion he showed. Even when I sat down next to him, he seemed stuck, didn't budge. We sat there in silence for a little while longer, because I was scared to ask him how he felt. This kind of stuff was out of horror movies. It wasn't supposed to be happening in real life, but it was. My life.

I didn't really know how to read him at this point. He might have wanted to leave or something and just didn't know how to say it.

"Journey, I had no idea you was going through all this. Why didn't you tell me?" he asked, looking like he was batting back tears. There were a lot of things I wanted to tell him but couldn't. Some things I might not ever be able to share.

"We've only been kicking it for a little while. I didn't know if we had that type of bond just yet."

He sat there contemplating his next statement for a little while longer, and I hoped to God I did the right thing. Khalid was the only person I had to talk to besides my mother, because Lord knows Vince was an asshole and didn't give a damn about anyone but himself.

"Journey, look at me," he said, turning my face toward his.

I felt like I was going to cry; I just didn't know what I was crying for. I'd been in this situation for so long that I was immune to any other feelings besides when it came to my mom. I gave my all to keeping my mother alive and staying alive myself. So many days I felt like I wanted to off both of us, so me and my mom wouldn't have to suffer anymore, but I learned in school that suicide sent you straight to the basement, and I didn't necessarily want to spend an eternity in hell either. Many days I wondered if being in hell would be better than the hell I was forced into here on earth, but I knew God only gave you what you could handle. I just didn't know how much longer I could handle it. Vince made sure of that, often saying he had to toughen me up for the streets because the streets didn't give a damn about a little girl who had a mom that was dying.

"I love you, Journey. Since the first time I saw you in class back in second grade, I knew you were going to be the one. We're in this together, okay?"

I was struck stupid. Has he been noticing me for that long? I had already been going to Evelyn Graves for two years before Khalid showed up, but he didn't seem to notice me until now. It was like I was invisible all of these years.

I shook my head like I understood what he was saying, but we would soon see if he was really ready to ride with me on this. I couldn't tell him just yet how things were between Vince and me because I still couldn't believe it myself, but one of these days, I would have to spill the beans. I honestly didn't think he could handle any more of my secrets today anyway. Or maybe he could, but could I trust him with knowing how Vince treated me? Could I tell him what my mouth had really experienced and we've already kissed? It was too painful for me to speak about, and I didn't think I could tell him without breaking down.

I sat closer to him on the couch so that we could watch some television before it was time for him to leave. I didn't know how long he was going to be able to stay, but I enjoyed him for as long as I could. We stretched out on the floor and watched *The Power Rangers*, and he pretended he was the green ranger and I was the pink one. Pokémon was one of our favorites too. It felt so good having him there.

I was going to call Vince to see how long he was going to let Khalid stay, but decided against it, because if I reminded him, he might just come and get him now. Instead, we went over some of the Bible verses that we had to learn in class, and he broke down the meanings for me, so that I could better understand them the way he did. We had children's Bibles given to us by the school, but even then sometimes it was a little challenging to get a grasp on what was being said.

It got dark fairly quickly, and I saw that it was almost eight o'clock and no one had come to check on him. I wondered briefly if he would be spending the night, but he didn't bring any changing clothes that indicated he would, so I knew someone would come eventually.

"Let me check on my mom," I said to Khalid before we started going over math problems. My English skills were the bomb; I just couldn't understand how angles were calculated and all that, but Khalid had it down pat, so I knew I would get it too. It was almost time to feed my mother as well for the night, so I would have to stop for a second to get her situated anyway.

When I walked into the room, I was expecting to see her coming out of her nod and watching television, because she loved *Wheel of Fortune* and *Jeopardy*. She looked strange from the door, but I couldn't really tell because all I was working with was the glare from the boob tube. For some reason, I felt like something was wrong, and I was scared to get closer to find out. Opting to use the lamplight instead of the ceiling, I got closer to my mother's bed so that I could see what was going on.

I jumped back when I turned the light on, not believing my eyes. My mom's eyes were rolled up into the back of her head, and all I could see were the whites of her eyes staring up at me. Her mouth was hanging wide open, with her tongue dangling out the side, and her skin looked gray. I didn't want to believe it, but when I leaned over to touch her arm, her skin felt cold and clammy.

"Please, Lord, don't do this to me," I said as I got up on the side of the bed and tried to prop my mother's body up. She couldn't be dead. I laid my head down on her chest to listen to her heart, and there wasn't a sound coming from her. I felt like the world was slowing down its rotation and we were coming to a screeching halt.

"Khalid! Khalid, call my uncle!" I said through tears as I tried to think of a way to get her heart back to pumping. My mother was dead, and I couldn't handle it.

"Journey, what's wrong?" Khalid asked as he ran to the bedroom door. I was in tears and could only see shadows. It felt like my heart would stop beating next, and I felt faint.

"Khalid, call my uncle. Call Vince. My mom is not breathing."

He ran out of the room in search of my cell phone, and did as I asked. Vince instructed me that if something ever happened to my mother,

I was to call him first, and he would call the ambulance once he got here. Khalid stood in the doorway and called my uncle's phone what felt like a hundred times before he answered.

I was crying hysterically by then, and all I could do was lay my head on my mother's stomach and rock back and forth, hoping once someone got here they would have time to save her. She couldn't be dead. Not right now. Not when I needed her the most.

It took Vince over half an hour to come to the crib, and by the time he got there, both Khalid and myself were crying and exhausted, not knowing what our next move should be. Vince was cursing up a storm and pushing us out of the room, and Khalid had to practically drag me out of the room by my feet because I refused to budge. Because of the storm, it took the ambulance just as long to get to where we were, and by the time they investigated the situation, my mother was pronounced dead.

Khalid sat and held me in the living room, my body shaking hard from all the crying I was doing. The ambulance drivers were not allowed to move the body until the coroner got there, and by then, everybody was out on the block to see what was going on. I didn't know where Mr. Joey was at. Even Choice and Bird were outside, but I couldn't have cared less at this point. As I listened to Vince fabricate a story about what happened to my mom for the police, I zoned out, trying to keep from going crazy.

My mother was all I had, and I was cool until they brought her body out of the room inside of a big black bag. I heard one of the EMTs say they had to peel her body from the bed because her flesh was stuck to it from all of the leaking sores she had all over it. The nurse that came here was supposed to dress all of her open wounds, but because of her illness, they weren't healing properly.

I watched them as they wheeled my mother out the door, and I said a silent good-bye to her and a prayer, because I knew Vince wouldn't do the right thing and bury her properly. This was my life, and for the first time, I was unsure about what tomorrow would bring.

Vincent Clayton

A Change of Plans

I swear shit happens at the most inopportune times. Why did this bitch have to go and die? Now I was gonna have to go down to child welfare and all that bullshit so they wouldn't put Journey's ass away in foster care. Shit, I needed her to cook this good product up, so she couldn't be put away. No one did the shit like she did. The only thing was now I ain't have nobody to test the shit out on, so I guess I'd have to keep giving away these freebies every so often to keep the shit poppin'.

I saw Journey crying on the couch, but I didn't bother to offer her any comfort. People die every day, and life goes on, so what was the tears about? Her ass would die one day, too, so she needed to get over it. Nobody was promised tomorrow, and that's a life lesson in itself.

Khalid looked at me like he hated me, but that little nigga was the least of my concerns. If he had an issue with the way shit was, he needed to talk to his damn daddy about that.

"Journey, let me talk to you for a minute," I said to her once the body was finally out of the house and things had settled down. Joey wasn't answering his phone, so Khalid was chilling until I was ready to take him around to his house. I started to let the little nigga walk by himself since he kept giving me the grizzly, but I knew Joey wouldn't do Journey like that, so I let him chill.

I waited for her to come into her mother's room while I cleaned out all of the product and money I had stashed in the house. I didn't know if child protective services would do a thorough search of the place, and I didn't need anything compromising my situation. We had money to make. I had Journey discard the works she used to fix her mother too. I'm not sure how much of an autopsy would be performed, but I didn't need any evidence lying around.

She came in looking like it was the end of the world for her, but by the time I was done with her, she wouldn't have a care in the world for anybody. Out in the streets, it's survival of the fittest, and your feelings could cost you your life at any given moment. A man that hesitates to pull the trigger is a dead nigga. That's the way the game is played.

"What's wrong with your face? Why are you looking like that?" I asked her after she took a seat on the edge of her mom's bed. You could still smell the stench of pus and dried blood coming from the bed, where they had to peel her body from the sheets. The health care worker that was supposed to be taking care of my sister-in-law would be coming out later to dispose of everything properly, so that no one would get sick. I already had plans to turn this room into a lab so that Journey wouldn't have to work out in the open on the kitchen table when she was cooking up product.

She didn't bother to respond, but her body shook slightly from the tears she was shedding, and it was getting on my damn nerves. I could go for some head at this moment to calm my damn nerves, but with the boy here and her all upset, I wouldn't even be able to enjoy the bullshit. I honestly didn't know what to say to her. My parents died from the same shit I hustled, so I didn't have anyone to teach me right from wrong. I had to just make shit fit the way I needed it to be.

"Journey, what did I tell you about how life works?" I asked her as I took a seat on the win-

dowsill and waited for her to recite the words I
made her study from day one.

"You said you live then you die. But Uncle
Vince, that doesn't stop it from hurting," she said
through her tears.

"True, but does it bring that person back?" I
asked her, so that she could see my point. People
die every second of every day, and more than
half of them aren't even missed.

"No," she said as she tried to dry her tears.

"So, there you have it. Go in the bathroom
and wash your face, and stop being so weak. You
wouldn't be able to break down like that on the
streets, so keep that in mind." Once she got herself together, I had her straighten up around the
house and help me carry my stuff down to the
first floor. Joey's knucklehead son could help me
take the shit to my Jeep, and then I would walk
him home. I knew leaving her in the house alone
was the wrong thing to do, but in the long run, it
would make her a stronger person. I just hoped I
didn't create a monster.

I grabbed up the two duffle bags and gave
Khalid one, and we made our way down the
street to my Jeep that was parked in front of
Choice's crib. There were big piles of snow everywhere, and the street had some major slippery spots, making it a little difficult for Khalid

to keep up with me, but he managed. He kept mean-mugging me on the way down, but I would lay his little ass out, along with his peoples, so I did my best not to let it faze me.

As we got closer to his house, I could hear Shanyce and Joey fighting like cats and dogs, but I didn't hesitate to knock on the door so that they could take their seed and I could be gone. Joey opened the door like he was ready to kill somebody, but when he saw his son standing there, he calmed down and looked at his watch.

"Yo, Vince, my bad, dude. I didn't know it got this late. Sorry he was around there for so long."

"It's cool. It was time for Journey to turn in, so I just walked him back. I'll see you on the block tomorrow, right?" I asked him as I turned to walk away, leaving out the intimate detail that my sister-in-law had died. I would just leave it up to Khalid to fill his dad in on the details, and I would handle it accordingly afterwards. He confirmed that he would be out tomorrow, if not later on tonight, and I left it at that and made my way around to the spot.

When I walked in, I stepped into the cipher while we watched the events that took place at my sister-in-law's house play out on the news. I knew I should be around there comforting Journey, but she had to grow up eventually.

I looked at my watch to check how much time I had, because I knew child protective services would be showing up to make sure she was cool. I knew I could trust Choice and Bird to run shit while I handled my business, because I figured I might have to stay around there for a couple of days. I would make it more comfortable for her to be in there, though. Chicks liked to shop, so I figured if I showed her a few magazines and helped her remodel, she'd be over her mom in no time and we could get back to business. I would give her a few days to grieve—I'm not totally heartless—but afterwards, I didn't want to hear shit else about it. Fiends don't get funerals, so I hoped she had her chance to say her good-byes before they took her mother's body out of the house.

"Yo, you cool, dude?" Choice asked me as he passed a lit blunt my way. I didn't feel any type of way about the situation, so it didn't really matter to me.

"Yeah, I'm good, playa. Another one bites the dust," I said, bringing a round of laughter from the crew. They already know how I felt about the death thing. I would just have to spend a little time down this end until the law felt like Journey was in a safe place. The crew would watch the spot when I was gone, so I wasn't really worried about it. They would make sure Journey was safe, if for nothing else than to protect the product we were moving.

Joey Street

Get In Where You Fit In

"You a fuckin' slut. The only reason I'm here is because of my son."

"You know what? Fuck you, Joey. The only reason I'm keeping you here is because of our son. After all I've done for you, this is how you treat me?"

"All you've ever done for me was fuck all my friends and spend all my money, and I'm tired of this shit."

We'd been arguing since I got back in the house, and of course, she tried to deny everything my son said. Why would my son have a reason to lie to me? Even the dude from the breakfast store hinted that he knew what her pussy looked like, so what was I supposed to do? I always knew Shanyce was a fast ass, but I figured if I wifed her and gave her everything she needed, she would calm down. Here we were nine and a half years later with a kid, and she was still on the same shit.

"I just told you he was fuckin' lying. What else do you want me to do?"

"Do you want me to go get Vince so that he could tell me what my bedroom looks like? Or what about half of Bartram Village? Do they know how we living up in this bitch too? I knew you was a whore when I fucked you, and the only reason why I stayed was because you took the abortion money I gave you and bought summer clothes instead of getting your ass up on the table."

That shit hurt her. I know it did. We'd been arguing that fact for years, even though I promised her years ago that I wouldn't throw that up in her face again, and that I had forgiven her. She trapped me, though, and being the man that I was, I wasn't going to let her ride out by herself, so we made it official. Or as official as it was going to get.

I put a ring on her finger, but we had yet to take the plunge, mostly because she was a damn whore and everybody knew it; so much so that I was thinking about getting a revolving door put on our bedroom to make access easier. Shit, you would think that she would want to do right in front of our son, so that he would have some morals. There was only so much that Christian school was going to teach him. He had to get the rest of his values from home, and the way shit was looking, if we had to depend on Shanyce, it wasn't going to happen.

"That's some hurtful shit to say, Joey. How could you really expect me to give up my son?"

"At the time, it was too early to even know we would have a son. You trapped me, and that's just the way it is."

She broke out in tears on me, and I tried to act like it wasn't fazing me, but it had my chest tight on some real shit. It's not like I didn't care about Shanyce, because I'd definitely grown to love her over the years; but she was making me look real stupid out in the street, and eventually I would have to put more bodies up under my belt if these niggas was going to be thinking I was on nut status. That's the shit she didn't understand.

I started to apologize, but for what? She was giving out coochie credit cards all over the damn place, with no regard to how it would affect our household. Fuck her, man. I had other shit to worry about, especially when they finally found her brother down the park. I was glad it stormed the way it did, because that would give me some time to get my game face together, but it was inevitable. I murdered her brother so that he wouldn't murder me. That's the way the game is played. Kill or be killed.

A knock on the door interrupted our battle briefly. I started to ignore it, but then I remembered my boy was out there and Vince was probably dropping him off. My speculation was correct. I opened the door and saw them standing there.

"Everything cool, man?" Vince asked as he tried to look around me and into the house. I ushered my son into the crib and pulled the door tighter because I was hot with his ass anyway, and I hadn't quite figured out how I would be dealing with him just yet.

"Yeah, everything good, playa. Thanks for walking Khalid home. I'll be out in a little while." I offered him the only explanation he needed. That was the problem: everybody in the neighborhood knew our damn business. I would be digging in Shanyce's ass about that as well. "Anytime, man. See you in a little while." He tried to steal one last glance around me, but I closed the door in his damn face. I wanted to curse Shanyce's ass out again, but when I got back to the living room, she was holding Khalid and crying.

"What's wrong?" I asked her, not sure if she was crying because of what I just said to her or if something else had gone down.

"Journey's mom died while Khalid was over there," she said through her tears, causing my mouth to drop open for the second time today. "What?"

"The ambulance was around there and everything. He said everything was cool, but when Journey went to check on her, she was dead."

Vince ain't bother to say a word to me about the shit. How fucked up is that? Yeah, I was gonna have to definitely step to dude about some shit, because apparently he thought he was untouchable. Why wouldn't he say something? If some shit had gone down while his niece was here, I would have told him. That made me wonder how much he really cared about the little girl, because on some real shit, he just recently started looking out for her.

She was kept a little on the raggedy side for a long minute, but I guess he decided to step up her game. It made me wonder what she had to do to get put on, though, because Vince did nothing for free. I knew he had a thing for young girls, too, but after he got caught with that sixteen-year-old last summer, I assumed he learned his lesson. The young girl's family whipped his ass for what seemed like hours, but when her mother tried to press charges, the girl denied being with him, and there was nothing they could do. The girl claimed she was in love with him. When she tried seeing him again and he brushed her off, it was too late. The judge wouldn't believe her, and he walked away scot free.

Shanyce had Khalid in the bed tucked in, and it killed me to see my boy in tears, but what could I do? I knew him and Journey had gotten tight, so seeing her in pain surely did something to him. I would talk to him tomorrow, since this incident was still fresh and he was still hurting from it.

I thought briefly about Journey and who she had to comfort her, but that wasn't my business to dip into. I just prayed that whatever hand she was dealt didn't harden her heart, because when they were changed around at her age, there was no turning back.

"Shanyce, we're not done talking," I said to her at my son's bedroom door, walking away to meet her in our bedroom. I couldn't help but think how Vince probably had her up in here, ass out. I knew she was a snake charmer, so nine times out of ten, she blessed him. That was part of the reason why I stopped kissing her years ago. When I first started hearing the rumors back in the day about her getting around, I deaded all affection besides the dick-down I gave her. I don't know whose nut was coating her tonsils at any given moment, and I preferred not to sample the shit to find out.

"Where did Khalid get the gun from, Joey?" she asked me when she came back into the room. I couldn't tell her that I had a stash in my son's closet, but that would be moved soon, because eventually she'd come across it and we would have yet another problem. "I don't know."

"So, it wasn't yours?" she asked with a hint of skepticism in her voice, letting me know up front that she didn't believe me. "No."

"Just get rid of it," she said in a defeated tone that said she didn't want to talk about it anymore. Neither did I, but our conversation was far from over.

I didn't bother to respond; I just grabbed my coat and bounced. I stopped by my son's room to check on him, and found him sitting in the window, crying. Stepping into the room completely, I closed the door behind me so that we could talk and not have his mom butt in.

"Dad, she just died out of nowhere," my son said to me when I sat down on the bed. He was crying so hard he was practically hiccupping, and it tore me up on the inside.

"Khalid, I know that was a lot for you to deal with, and it'll get better in time."

"But what happens to Journey, Dad? Who is going to help her get through this?"

For the first time in a long time, I didn't have an answer for him. I couldn't reassure him that things would go right for her, because that little girl lost her mother, and was now out there to fend for herself. That could make her or break her, and I hoped she was a strong one.

I consoled my son as best as I could, and I sat there until he fell asleep. I didn't even bother to check on Shanyce, because I was two steps from strangling her ass anyway.

When I got around the block, Vince, Bird, and Choice were sitting in a cipher on the porch, so I joined them, drowning my troubles in weed smoke. We were all silent for a while, I suppose just thinking about the events that took place this evening and what we had to do. I knew if nothing else, I had to stack my chips fast and bounce.

"So, you ready to get this money?" Vince asked me, eyeing me curiously.

"Never been more ready in my life."

"Cool. We got some shit we need you to take care of, and we didn't forget about that nigga Bunz, either. We gonna let him ride for a while since shit is quiet right now, but he gonna get his. Right now, it's time to get that paper," Vince said, speaking for the group.

It was time to step the game up, whether I was ready or not. I didn't plan to stay in the game that much longer, but who ever does? All I knew was shit was about to change, but I doubted it would be for the better. I had to get in where I fit in, and if that meant bumping some soldiers out, then I guess that's how it had to be.

Bird pulled out a bottle of Mad Dog 20/20 and we took turns sipping from the bottle, trying to keep warm. It was sad that I would rather drink after my boys than tongue-kiss my girl, but that was the reality we lived in. All I could do was see where it took me. Right now, I was focused on getting this paper before this paper chase got the best of me.

Part Two

Thanks to the duffle bag, the brown paper bag,
the Nike shoe box for holding all this cash . . .
—*Jay-Z*

Five Years Later . . .

Journey Clayton

My How Time Flies

I barely know how I had survived since my mom died. I mean, so much had happened since then. Vince moved in for a little while so that I wouldn't be forced into foster care, and it was like having the devil himself residing under this roof. The only thing that came out of it that was any good was that since he stayed here most nights, he kept food in the house. That was only because his simple ass had to eat too.

Surprisingly, he was a little more lenient as I got older, though. Like, where before he would drive me to Toya's house to get my hair done, now he would let me walk over to the projects by myself, as long as I got my hair done early in the day and Toya didn't take forever doing my hair. I was cool with that, though.

The only thing I hated was how the guys out there looked at me, like I was a piece of meat

they were just waiting to pounce on. Especially
this guy named Bunz. His look made my skin
crawl, and not in a good way. He would always
flick his tongue at me and blow me kisses. Yuck!
All that did was make me walk faster.

I was starting to blossom as well, and my once
boyshaped body was turning into a round booty
that jiggled in my sweat pants when I walked. My
days of wearing a training bra were gone, going
right into cute little pushup bras from La Perla.

I overheard my uncle and Mr. Joey talking out
on the stoop one night about how they were going to kill Bunz from some beef they had back in
the day. They had been on to Bunz for years, and
a part of me thought Mr. Joey was just scared to
do it. He was supposed to be so spectacular at his
"job," so I couldn't understand why he hadn't put
Bunz in the ground by now. Or maybe Bunz was
even better at not getting caught.

I cried and cried for what seemed like years after my mom passed, but never in front of Vince.
If he saw me crying, he would go straight the hell
off for hours, and I eventually learned to control
my emotions around him. At first he would let
me get off and cry and scream, but pretty soon, if
I even looked like I might think about shedding
a tear, he was on my neck. I can remember one
time when I cried, he made me squat down in

the corner and hold three Yellow Pages phone books out in front of me. Every time I dropped the books, he added five minutes onto my time. It wasn't until I could barely stand and only really had an hour to get rest before I had to get up for school that he let me lie down.

What pissed me off the most was when he punished me in that way and his friends were over at the house. They would be loud and obnoxious, and I could barely breathe through all the weed smoke. I was just a child, though, so there wasn't really much I could do except what I was told. Khalid helped me tremendously throughout everything

I'd gone through, and he drilled in me all those Bible verses to help me stay strong and look forward to the day when I would be on my own and away from Vince. He was going to be the first black president and I'd be his wife, the first lady. Our friendship grew and matured over the years, and we told each other everything—except what Vince did to me sometimes. I still couldn't say it out loud to anyone. The only person I talked to about it was God, and more often than not, I wondered if He heard my prayers.

I learned in school that everything we did in life was a lesson learned, and we were supposed to grow from it and learn how to better deal with recurring situations. Nothing could be worse than this, though.

I did have another secret I couldn't tell Khalid, only because that person swore me to secrecy. Also because I knew it would hurt him too bad, and I didn't want him to feel the kind of pain I felt on a daily basis. To know that no one in your family loves you was heavy. Not one single person on my mother's side or my dad's. I was literally in the world by myself. Wow, I didn't think it was possible, but this was the life I lived every single day.

So I did my job. I got up and went to school, came home, and cooked and bagged the coke, made sure Vince and whoever was over ate dinner; then, if I was allowed to go to sleep, I did that until the next day, when I started from scratch all over again.

I missed my mom. Every day I wondered what my life would have been like had she not gotten hooked on drugs and later contracted AIDS. Would I have had a loving family where I was invited to my cousin's birthday parties, or had parties of my own? I couldn't remember one time receiving a hug from my mom or dad, or either one of them telling me they loved me. I had vague memories of my mother's mom, and even that memory wasn't a pleasant one. I blocked out a lot of my earlier years, so even if one of my family members walked up and slapped me in the face, I wouldn't know who they were.

I often dreamed about running away, but where would I go? Anywhere would be better than here, but I wasn't so sure sometimes when I saw the nightly news and heard the stories of kids in foster care. The world just seemed full of bad people, so I figured I'd be better off dealing with Vince. At least with him I knew what and whom I was dealing with. Right now, I had to finish bagging up these tops so that I could go to sleep. I assumed Vince was out for the night, and most times, if I was already in bed, he would let me be; other times, he would invade my body. I wasn't sure what tonight would bring, but like so many others, I just wanted to make it to the morning.

Bunz B

Honey Bunz

"I'ma need you to hold your fuckin' head steady and stop all that gagging. You fuckin' up my flow. Shit, didn't you say you was a pro at this shit?"

I had this young trick over here sucking my dick for the past half hour, and I just couldn't bust this nut. She was a little younger than I like, but she'd been sweatin' me for a minute, so I decided to take the plunge and let her rock the mic, and that was the biggest mistake I ever made. I was just gonna let her give me some head and roll, but I was gonna have to beat the guts up anyway if we were ever going to get anywhere with this. I felt almost bad even thinking about it because she couldn't be no more than seventeen, but she came up in here on some grown woman shit, so I was definitely going to let her cash that check her young ass wrote out.

Her face looked like she was in pain, and I know her jaws had to be stiff as shit by now, 'cause your boy working with some shit. I had a tight grip on her weave, to keep her head from moving too much while I fucked her mouth like I was beatin' the pussy up. She looked like she was two strokes from throwing up, but she knew better. I was going to get that nut if it was the last thing I did that day.

In all honesty, the real reason why I couldn't concentrate was because I had too many niggas on my head trying to settle beef, and I didn't really have the manpower to handle it all. After that popcorn-ass robbery Street and I did back in '98, it was some bullshit ever since. I mean, shit, it was 2003. When was niggas gonna let bygones be bygones?

I chanced a glance down, trying to decide what position I was going to put her in first. If her teeth scraped against my dick one more time, though, it was going to be a problem, so I decided to let her up before shit got intense.

"Strip naked and get on the floor," I said to her after I pulled my dick from her lips and let go of her head. She looked relieved as she got up to do what I said. Little did she know she would wish I had bust that good nut in her mouth, because I was going to have to put it in her ass.

Taking a good look at her body, I noticed right away that she had it going on for her to be so young and tender. Her breasts sat up nice and perky, and were more than a handful. Her stomach was flat, and her sides curved out like a CocaCola bottle. When she turned around and bent over to pull her pants down, I saw that her ass was huge and looked soft and fluffy. My dick was as hard as Chinese algebra, and I knew I was about to tear some shit up.

She lay down on the floor, looking like she was ready for me, but what she didn't know was she'd probably be getting up with more than just a wet pussy. I fucked all bitches raw, so there was no telling what I had going on; but if she didn't inquire, I wasn't telling. She had a smile on her face at the moment, but all that would be changing momentarily.

I got down on the floor with her and flipped her ass right over, pulling her ass up in the air doggy style so that I could dive right in. This simple bitch was moanin' and playing with her clit like she couldn't wait for me to get in. Working up a gob of spit, I hawk-spitted on the crack of her ass, and she jumped when it landed and rolled down her ass crack. She started swerving her hips and pushing her ass further up in the air like I was getting ready to get up in her pussy, but I grabbed her hips and held her steady, driving my dick in her asshole real quick, causing her to lose her bowels all over my dick.

She tried to scream, but her voice got caught in her throat as I rammed in and pulled out of her at a rapid speed. There was shit and blood all over both of us, but I wasn't stopping until I came, and she just had to deal with it. She started screaming, begging me to pull my dick out, but I wasn't about to do anything like that. She tried to crawl away, but the grip I had on her hair kept her steady—or else she would have pulled all her tracks out, and I doubted she would.

"Omar, please. I can't take it!" she screamed out, using the fake name I gave her when I met her a while back. I acted like I didn't understand English while I kept up my pace until the cream started building up on the tip of my dick.

"Shut up, bitch. This what you wanted, ain't it?" I sped up my pace, practically killing her simple ass to the point where she couldn't even scream anymore. She just tried to take it. I was practically putting my balls in her; that's how hard I was hitting that shit. After a few more pumps, I pulled out and jerked my dick, busting all over her hair and back, and then fell back on the floor to rest my legs. It took me a minute to get my head on straight, and that's when I realized she was crying. This bitch was about to fuck my whole day up, and I wasn't having it.

"Yo, get the fuck up and go wash up. Bring me a hot, soapy rag out when you done."

She hesitated for a minute, but after I kicked her on the side, she got up and limped to the bathroom. Blood was still trickling out of her ass, but I figured she'd be cool after she washed up. I took a moment to get my head together, and while she was in the shower, I used the sink to wash off the remnants of our activity, because I didn't feel like waiting for her to get done to bring me a rag. I didn't have time to take a shower. I had to go back out there and get on that grind.

By the time she came out, I was dressed and ready to go. I threw a couple of dollars on the floor at her feet, but she ignored it and put her clothes back on, walking ahead of me to leave. I noticed blood starting to seep through the jeans she had on, so I ushered her ass out a little faster so that she could get gone. I must have really put a hurting on her ass, literally, so I knew not to expect her around me anymore.

Once we got outside, she went one way and I went the other, so that I could see what was up with my boys for tonight. We had been scoping out this little black-owned convenience store in West Philly for a while that we was thinking about hitting up, and I was trying to convince them to do the shit tonight.

It was run by a Muslim woman. We didn't really fuck with them niggas because they ran too deep, but I was willing to take the chance just to get this money. I was tired of the stick-up kid bullshit I was doing, and I knew they had enough gwap in that store to set me up for a nice little minute. I could take that money and jet down to Maryland for a while until shit died down. I had a few cousins down there that would put me on for a while.

"So, what time we riding out?" I asked my right hand man, Gary. This nigga stayed high off them damn pills, so I don't even know how he functioned on a day to day basis, but he always got the job done.

"In a little while. It's dark now, but the store don't close 'til like eleven, so we need to be getting there around that time. We need this to go as smooth as possible, and no killing people tonight, Bunz. We just gonna get the money and jet."

"Whatever, nigga. You just do what you gotta do." We stood around smoking an L for a while, while I thought about how I was going to ditch this body I had in the trunk of my car. I had the nigga in there for like three days now, and it was bound to start stinking sooner than later, so I had to do something quick. I figured I could get these dudes to help me ditch it after we got done with this robbery, but I couldn't tell them what was up now, because I knew they would bitch up.

I dipped back to the crib and grabbed my duffle bag so that we could get shit poppin'. I had a shotgun that was sawed off down to the barrel, an AK-47, and about three 9 mm's that we would use to do the job. I was going to bring the hand grenades I copped from my Puerto Rican friend, Jesus, but I figured we didn't need all that. Hopefully they would just give up the goods willingly and we would be cool. We had ski masks, and the serial numbers were shaved off the weapons, so as long as no one made any stupid mistakes, we would be good.

"Y'all niggas ready to ride out?" I asked them when I got back up the hill, and in response, they all piled in. Jamel and Kev were in the back, me and Gary in the front, and we moved toward the West Side to make this shit happen.

The weed smoke was so thick in the car that when I pulled up to the light and rolled the window down, a thick cloud of white smoke rushed out the window and toward the sky, clearing all of our vision for a second. I popped like four Xanies to get my mind right, so that by the time we finished up in here, I'd be zoned out.

We was riding to *Many Men* by the boy 50 Cent that had just come out, and the lyrics to this song hit home like a mutha. Plenty of niggas wanted me dead, but they had to catch me first. It's hard to grab a man that moves in the shadows. Fuck all of 'em.

I was thinking about all kinds of shit, and although it had been a while, I still owed Joey a visit too. I wouldn't directly come at him, though. His son looked like he was ready for the streets, and I started when I was about his age, so I would be the perfect person to put him on. Shit, his secret was safe with me, because I knew what he was tryin'a do. He had Vince's pretty-ass niece on his hip, so I knew he was trying to floss her, and I would make it my business to show him the ropes so that he could make it happen. Fuck Joey. I'd deal with him when the time came.

When we pulled up to the store, I left the car idling across the street at an angle where we could see right in. The only Muslim brother that was in the store rolled out about ten minutes after we pulled up, leaving only two women in the store. I was already on my dip because those pills I took started working faster than they normally did. My head felt heavy as shit, but we had a job to do, so there was no turning back. "This gonna be easier than I thought," I said more to myself, drawing a quiet chuckle from the crew. We waited a while longer to make sure he wouldn't double back and that no one else was watching the store, before we decided to make a move.

"Get y'all shit together, and let's go in loaded. It's about time to make that move."

The crew passed the duffle bag around, each grabbing a gun and a mask before we got out. We wouldn't pull the masks all the way down until we got into the store, and everyone knew their position, so it was on. We waited until the clock said ten-fifty, then we made our move. They locked the door at exactly eleven, so we had to be swift. "Okay, men, let's make this happen."

We made our way across the street, and I just prayed that everything went right, because we only had one shot, and hopefully we wouldn't have to kill the witnesses.

Too many dead bodies under my belt kept me from sleeping most nights. I never thought it would happen, but the nightmares happened more often than I liked to admit. And just keeping my back guarded from Joey and Vince was enough to handle without being tired from the night before. Joey was nice with his shit. That's why I was surprised I was still walking around this joint. That was part of the reason why I hadn't tackled Vince's niece yet. I knew if I even stepped sideways to her, my ass was grass.

These Muslim dudes, though, them niggas was not to be fucked with. They would have the Ville turned upside down for real if shit got out of hand and they knew I was behind it. Vince and Joey were a problem, but they were more like annoying flies compared to the dragons that called themselves Muslims. They ran deep, and I felt bad for anyone who had to feel the wrath come down on them. That's why I had to play this shit close, and hope this thing went smoothly. I couldn't afford for it not to.

Journey Clayton

Not So Sweet Fourteen

"Got me lookin' so crazy right now. Your love's got me lookin' so crazy right now."

You couldn't tell me I didn't have a body like Beyoncé. At the tender age of almost fourteen, I'd filled out nicely, with full C-cup breasts and an hourglass shape that curved out into a nice round booty. I stood at a smooth five foot four inches, and everything was proportioned perfectly. I was killing the game and I knew it. My hair had gotten to be down to the middle of my back, and I kept it in soft curls that framed my face thanks to Toya, who had been doing my hair since I was nine years old. Bald bitches would always hate and say I had a weave, but they knew that there wasn't a track in sight. They just couldn't stand the fact that I looked so fly.

I loved this hairstyle because it made me look like I was part Dominican or something, and not like I had a Just For Me relaxer kit keeping my roots under control. Some said I resembled a slightly darker version of the actress that played Ashley Banks from one of my favorite shows, *The Fresh Prince of Bel Air*. Toya made me look like we had the same texture of hair, but I thought I was cuter. I had all the moves from the videos down to a science, and I swore I was doing the shit better than Beyoncé herself as I rolled my hips and flung my hair around like I was in the video.

I would be lying if I said I didn't notice all the stares I got when I walked through the hood, but since day one, my heart belonged to Khalid, and that's where it would stay. He was going to be the first black president, and I could picture myself standing by his side while he ran the country. The thought always put a smile on my face. Thanks to him, my grades had gotten a lot better, too, and together I felt like we were invincible.

I would be turning fourteen in a few days, and I was so excited because I planned to give Khalid my virginity. He had waited so patiently all these years, and since I knew we were going to spend the rest of our lives together, I figured why wait? We paid extra close attention in health class, and at the free clinic, they didn't ask any question as to why we wanted birth control. They gave it to us willingly, so we were set. I was so excited and nervous at the same time, but I wouldn't want it to be anyone else, so it didn't matter.

I came up in the game since back in the day, too. I got so good at cooking up the Snow White that my uncle and his friends hustled that it only took me half the time to cook twice as much as before. Apparently, the fiends were loving it.

In the midst of all that, my wardrobe grew extensively, and with the guidance of Toya, I had everything a girl could want, from Gucci bags to La Perla lingerie to Seven jeans and Citizens of Humanity tees. I was rocking Juicy Couture charm bracelets and all that, and everyone was hating because I was the only one in my class with Gucci sneakers, and it ate all them haters up on the inside—especially Gina.

I was still performing tricks for my uncle, and since my taste got to be so expensive, so had his demands. He let me wear thongs and everything, so I looked to Toya for guidance, and made sure my bra and panties matched on a daily, even though no one saw them but me.

Vince still hadn't penetrated me yet, but his promise to take me at fourteen never left my head, and that's why it was so important to me to give it to Khalid first, before my uncle Vince had a chance to ruin the only gift I could give the man

I loved. I guess Vince kept doing the things he did to me now as payment for keeping me out of foster care. My mom was dead, so I didn't need the product anymore. He made me cook and bag it up to earn my keep, so what other reason could there be? Now, I'm not going to act like I totally hated the feeling I got when Vince went down on me. I had actually orgasmed a couple of times against my will. The only good thing was that I hoped to be able to show Khalid a few of my uncle's tricks so that when we did do our thing, it would be good for both of us.

I never got around to telling him how things were with me and my uncle, and I was hoping I would never have to. A part of me thought Vince would just stop on his own, but I wouldn't find out until much later that it would never happen that way.

Once the video ended, I still hummed the beat as I dug out some change from the bottom of the Fendi I was carrying, so that I could satisfy my craving for some Homegirls potato chips from the corner store. I was certainly enjoying my summer vacation so far, and actually couldn't wait until tonight. I was able to talk Vince into letting me go see *Final Destination 2* with Khalid. It had come out two weeks ago, and after too many nights of rough "almost" sex and oral pleasure, Vince finally okayed me to go.

Grabbing my keys off the coffee table, I checked my appearance in the wall mirror before stepping outside. I looked more than cute in a pair of light gray cotton Daisy Duke shorts that just barely covered my ass, and a pink baby tee that just met my belly button, both compliments of Old Navy. I slid my feet into my pink, gray, and black flip-flops that I had just gotten from Victoria's Secret a day ago, and I ensured that my bubble gum pink toenail polish wasn't chipped as I applied lip gloss to my lips and fluffed my hair one last time. I had to make sure I was on point, because you never knew who you would run into. Toya taught me that a long time ago.

Once outside, the humidity slapped me in my face as I graced Grays Avenue with my presence. There were a few hustle boys on the corner that stopped dead in the middle of their craps game to watch my ass bounce in my shorts as I crossed the street. They especially enjoyed the view when I dropped one of my quarters in the street and revealed my thong as I bent to pick it up. Vince put so much fear in everyone that no one would dare approach me, except for Bunz's simple ass, but we all knew he was a little nutty, so I didn't think much of it.

It was cold in the store. I wanted a blue freeze pop, so I put my hand across my chest to cover my erect nipples from the cold when I dipped in the freezer to get my frozen treat. I had on my figure eight earrings and Khalid's gold chain around my neck, and it felt like all eyes were on me as I made my way back across the street to go in. Vince told me to never wear my jewelry outside when I was by myself because Bartram Village bred a lot of stick-up kids, but it was broad daylight, and although I was conscious of my surroundings, I didn't think anyone would do anything.

"Damn, girl. I know you taste as sweet as you look," one of the guys said to me on the corner when I got on my side of the street. I chanced a glance at him, and he wasn't bad looking at all. The fact that he was holding his dick like it would fall off totally turned me off though, and instead of responding, I made a mad dash for the crib, being sure to lock the door behind me before I went upstairs.

I already had my outfit laid out, and I was nervous because although Khalid genuinely liked what I wore all the time, I wanted to look extra cute for our date. I had a cute pastel sundress from my favorite clothing store, Theory, that was swirled with pink, yellow, light blue, and white to match the pastel pink and yellow sandals and bag I got from Kate Spade. My breasts sat up perky, so I would only have on the dress and the shoes, not even a thong underneath.

Running all hot water in the tub, I let the tub fill while I made me a grilled cheese sandwich and cleaned up my mess. I watched an episode of *Martin* while I cooked up what was left of the product Vince had laid out for me, giving my bath water time to cool down to a nice temperature before I got in. It was almost eight o'clock, and I wanted to be dressed and ready for my nine o'clock date with my boo. I didn't want him to have to wait for me.

It didn't take me long to cap up and bag what I cooked, and I made sure to lock everything in the floor safe that Vince had built into the living room closet to keep everything hidden. Racing toward the bathroom, I didn't take as much time as I would have liked to soak, but I did rid myself of any pubic and underarm hair that was present on my body before I scrubbed my body from head to toe, until I sparkled like a new penny. I was often teased about my dark complexion, but nowadays, men seemed to love my brown skin.

I got out of the tub and dripped a trail of water toward my bedroom, where I took my time drying off and caressing parts of my body, pretending Khalid was there exploring me. I loved my own scent, and could smell my wetness as my fingers got lost between my folds. Through half-closed eyelids, I envisioned how I would look in my dress, although I'd tried it on a million times since I got it.

I felt like someone was watching me, and when I got up the nerve to look, my uncle Vince was standing in my doorway. The clock showed that I only had forty-five minutes before Khalid got there, so I hoped my uncle would just leave so that I could get dressed and be outside waiting for him. When I went to sit up, my uncle took three giant steps across the room, demanding me to lie back down. I wanted to cry, but tears were for weak bitches, and I was strong—or so I kept telling myself.

"Don't rush to get up because I'm here. I just want to taste your temperature," my uncle said to me in a lust-filled voice. I hoped like hell that he wouldn't try to have sex with me tonight. I didn't want his hands on me, and I didn't want his tongue anywhere near me, but if I tried to stop him, he would probably make me cancel my date with Khalid, and I was not trying to hear that.

Vince stood and looked at me like he was struggling with demons on the inside. I could see it in his eyes that he wanted to take it, and I hoped he could see in my eyes that I really didn't want him to. We locked eyes for what felt like forever before he decided to walk away and let me be.

It wasn't until I heard the door lock that I got up and ran in the bathroom to wash Vince's scent and saliva off me. I willed myself not to cry as I moisturized my body with pink grapefruit lotion from Carol's Daughter, afterward spritzing my body with Light Blue by Dolce and Gabbana because I loved the way the two citrus scents meshed together. Stepping into my dress, I decided to at least go with a thong as a precaution to soak up any juices later on. I knew how wet I could get, and Khalid could have me like a running faucet in the snap of a finger.

I still had a few minutes before Khalid got there, so I took the time to make sure my room was in tip top shape, just in case we came back here tonight. I practically lived by myself, with Vince only coming to check on me to pick up product and molest me on occasion. I never worried about how the bills were being paid because he pretty much took care of everything. So if me and Khalid did come back here, we would be alone.

Looking at the clock again, I was a little disappointed that Khalid didn't show up a little early, but I knew he would be here. He said he would call me when he was coming around the corner, and he'd never stood me up before, so I would just wait. I was a bundle of nervous energy, and I was ready to get this date started. I knew going out tonight I would still be a girl, but by morning, I planned to be a woman, and Khalid would make that happen for me before it was too late.

Shanyce Davidson

Rose-Colored Glasses

It was a damn shame how Vince treated that girl. Although I didn't have any concrete proof, I could almost bet my life that he was molesting her or some shit like that with his trifling-ass self. I swear I hated just looking at him, though I must admit that the dick-down was serious. A woman always knows, though, and I could tell by the way she carried herself that some shit was going on in there. She just seemed too damn timid for me, like she was scared or some shit. She was nothing like the other fast-ass little girls that lived around here, but she didn't come off as a typical child her age, either.

I knew Joey was about tired of my ass, too, because I fucked up his money in a major way the last time I took some out of the stash, and I didn't know how long it was gonna take to bounce back. I was hoping I could put some of the shit back, or even blame it on Khalid, but the amount that was missing was too big, and my heart wouldn't let me get my boy in trouble.

I shouldn't have taken so much, but I needed it. I told my young buck from down the bottom that I would look out for him, and he was on my heels about the cash I promised him, so I had no choice. On the real, Vince got me turned out on that shit—and the dick . . . I didn't know which one I be wanting more. I wasn't strung out like I was a crack head or some shit. I mean, I still looked good, my body was still on point, and I still went to work on a daily, but sometimes I'd be sitting at my desk and it was hard to concentrate on registering patients when all I could think about was my next hit of Snow White.

It was a shame, though, such a pretty little girl being corrupted by the hood. She was supposed to have a loving family to turn to, since both of her parents were taken out by the same drug that I loved, but all she had was trifling-ass Vince, with his big-dick self. I got a twinge in my pussy every time I thought about him.

Lately, we'd been getting more sloppy with our shit. I'd been letting Vince dip in my cookie jar for years, and Joey never knew, but when Khalid started running his mouth about him being around, we had to slow down.

I owed Joey, though. Rumor had it that he was the one who murdered my brother back in '98, and a part of me believed the rumor was true. Joey was known for ditching bodies down Bartram's Garden, but no one could ever pinpoint him on the shit, because he never left any tracks.

It wasn't until the snow had melted and spring emerged that a jogger discovered my brother's body early in the morning, but by that time, he had decomposed quite a bit, and we could only identify him by his dental records. When we went to view his body, it looked like a bag of rotten lunchmeat sitting up on the table. It wasn't even enough left to really cremate him. When I asked Joey about it, he denied it, but I knew better, because back in the day, me and Joey used to sit up and talk all night when his nightmares got to be too much and he wouldn't dare close his eyes.

He was just kind of quiet now, not really saying much, and he seemed kind of jumpy. The few times I mentioned not seeing my brother around before his body was discovered, he would just say shit like my brother was a junkie and he'd pop up soon enough. What I didn't know was that he would pop up dead, but I believe Joey did know.

At the funeral, I fell out like my life was over and acted a plum fool. It was partly from guilt, because I knew that I shouldn't have left him in here knowing Joey kept his stash in the crib and my brother was a crack head. Did I feel he had to die for that shit, though? Hell no, and I was tired of these half-baked niggas walking around Southwest playing God and shit like they had the right. On the flip side of that, though, when you do dirt, you get that shit, and my brother had being doing dirt longer than dirt would be doing him. I just hoped my son took another road and didn't follow behind this hustler mentality that Joey and me had. He was tough, but he wasn't built for the street life.

"Ms. Jackson, please come to the registration desk." I hated my damn job with a passion. I didn't always, though. Back in the day when I first started working there, it was a nice middle class neighborhood with working women who came in to get their yearly check-ups and birth control refills. Occasionally you'd find a shy housewife who, come to find out, was not so shy. Those ones were usually trying to hide the fact that they were creeping with their neighbor's husband and got burned, and they were trying to fix the issue before their husbands got back in town. But that was the most excitement we would get.

When the office started accepting C.H.I.P., all this shit went downhill, and now the office was filled with a ton of young girls getting treated for the same recurring STD every two weeks because they weren't smart enough to know that their dude of the moment had some shit. It was always the same story: since she "loved" him so much, he didn't have to use protection.

The girl that was sitting at my desk now smelled like trash truck juice on a hot July day, and it made me wonder what took her so long to come in for treatment.

"Is all of your information the same, Ms. Jackson?" I asked her as I typed past the patient demographics screening, knowing that the projects would be her home for generations to come. Not too many people left the Ville. They would contribute generations to an already depressing situation. I kept my son as far away from Bartram Village as I could. He would be better if it killed me.

"Yeah. My phone got cut off, but it'll be back on next week, so you can leave that number in there," she said as she brushed her bangs from her eyes with the longest fingernails I'd ever seen. I just shook my head in wonderment at how she could even function with them that long.

It took everything in me to keep a straight face, because for the life of me, I couldn't understand how her home phone wasn't working when welfare paid for every damn thing, and her rent was probably no more than twelve dollars a month. As illiterate and as ghetto as she carried herself, though, she had the Gucci hobo bag and the shoes to match that I wanted. The bag alone had to run her at least seven-fifty from Saks.

Her hair was laid with that new terra weave that everyone was wearing now, and her nails and toes looked freshly done. My only question was, who gets dressed like that to come to the damn clinic? What was this, the new club family center?

I was just tired, but I was more tired of having to wait for a hit. I had a small top in my bag that I could do in the bathroom real fast that would hold me over until I got down the way, so I rushed through her registration so that I could dip off real fast.

"Have a seat in the waiting room, Ms. Jackson. We'll be calling you back in a minute."

I had to hold my breath as her funky-ass got up out of the chair and sashayed her ass back to the waiting area as if her pussy didn't smell like death done twice. Turning my desk light off, I grabbed my bag real fast and dipped to the bathroom, letting my co-worker know that I would be right back.

On the low, I kept my work with me. I just grabbed a new syringe this week from the supply closet, so I was cool on that, and once I got myself comfortable in the handicap stall and found a lighter in the bottom of my bag, I was good. I used the veins in the back of my knees so that no one would see any track marks, and I always kept a bottle cap and cotton balls so that I could cook up anywhere when necessary. So much had happened in the past five years that I needed something to keep myself sane. With Joey and Vince going at it with Bunz all the time, and Khalid being so concerned with Journey, I often wondered who was concerned about me. Joey didn't even really show any interest in me like he used to. He would have sex with me sometimes just to shut me up so that he could try to get some sleep. The world I used to know was just crumbling around me, so I had started getting high more than usual.

My hands began to shake from the anticipation, and I had to try to calm myself down so that I wouldn't drop my shit. I wouldn't do a whole syringe, just enough to get me nice until I left. I still had to function, and didn't want to be on tilt at the desk.

Tapping out a little of the drug, I cooked it up real quick and pulled it up into the syringe, a small smile spreading across my face. Quickly finding a vein behind my knee, I injected the drug into my system, setting everything on the windowsill afterward.

Tears began to escape my eyes as I thought about what I just did and how it would affect my son if he ever found out. I told myself I could stop anytime I wanted to, but in reality, I didn't think I could. If I got help, that would be admitting I had a problem. I tried to convince myself that it wasn't that serious. I was a recreational user. I only wanted to get high sometimes, but I didn't necessarily need it—or so I thought.

It wasn't until after the spinning stopped and I could kind of see straight that I tried getting myself together. I heard a couple of my co-workers come into the bathroom, so I made sure I had all my shit before I walked out of the stall. They looked at me like they hated me, and I knew it was because I stayed fly, so fuck all of them. Just because I worked there didn't mean I couldn't afford to have nice shit, and I wasn't about to fuck up my high thinking about it.

I heard them say some smart shit as the door was closing behind me as I left out, not realizing that I had been gone for almost twenty minutes.

But I was cool. Jumping back into my work, I scheduled patient after patient until it was almost time for me to go.

At the end of the day, I made sure all of my charts were up in medical records, and I bounced out five minutes early, eager to get me some shit before I went in. I didn't want to dip in Joey's stash again, so I'd have to take a trip up west to cop. It wasn't Snow White, but it would do.

Khalid Street

Last Time

"When you gonna leave that little girl alone and start messing with a real woman? You know I liked you since like the first grade."

I knew I was dead wrong being up in here with Gina, but on some real shit, I really thought she called me over here because she wanted help with her math. She had to go to summer school because she failed algebra, and although I wasn't on nerd status, everyone knew math was my shit. I also knew that she had been trying to get at me since forever, but Journey had my heart, and I made sure everyone knew that.

That definitely didn't keep chicks from trying, though, and it was hard having to bat pussy off you all day when your own girl wasn't giving it up. I told Journey I would wait for her, and we promised that we would be each other's first, but I had Gina pressing her wetness against me through my sweat pants, and it was hard as hell to control an erection in a situation like this.

"Gina, I came to help you with your math, and you know I'm not leaving Journey, so why do you keep asking?"

"Because I know she not giving it up to you. I'm soft and wet with a tight grip, though. Don't you want to know what all the hype is about?"

I did want to know, but I didn't need to feel it to find out. All my homeboys done tapped it and told me what it was hitting for already, and they said I'd be better off getting some head, because the pussy was already worn out. When you're pretty like Gina, everyone wants you, and her low self-esteem–having ass gave it up willingly. I wasn't cool on getting sloppy seconds, thirds, fifths, or however many were before me.

Just the thought of it made my dick go back down, and I pushed her back off me gently as not to hurt her feelings. I had to get my shit together so that I could go see my girl.

"Actually, I'll pass on the hype, but when you're ready to get those numbers right, let me know," I said to her as I stood up and adjusted my dick in my boxers before smoothing my shirt out. I would have to go home and change before I saw Journey because I didn't want her smelling Gina all over me, especially since I didn't get none.

"So, you mean to tell me that you gonna pass up all this?" she asked as she stepped out of her short skirt, revealing the fact that she had on no panties underneath. Next came her shirt, and her braless breasts did look delectable. She had smooth, light skin, with dark nipples and a hairless pussy. I did think twice about doing a smash and grab, but that would just be something for her to throw in Journey's face, and I wasn't about to put my girl through that kind of bullshit.

"I'm good, ma. Trust." She looked disappointed as I walked out the door, but I had no control over that. Bitches are scandalous, and I knew my girl was well worth the wait.

Taking a peek at my watch, I put a little pep in my step because I was already running a little late, and I usually showed up early for our dates. Journey said she had a surprise for me, and I knew she was going to be looking real sexy. That alone put a smile on my face. When you got the baddest chick in the neighborhood on your arm and no one can get next to her, it feels good. Gina was only hot because she was giving it up to any and every body. Journey had class and sex appeal about her that made her stand out. I loved it.

I was a little later than I normally was because when I got home, I had to deal with my mom's shit. I knew she was getting high, but she kept denying it. Her and my dad were going through it right now because she dipped in his stash again, and I heard him asking my grandmom if she could keep some stuff at her house, because he couldn't trust my mom to leave his stuff here anymore.

It was crazy, because my dad was known for being one of the highest paid hit men in the area. That's why I couldn't understand why we were still living around here. At the same time, I didn't want to leave Journey, so I just dealt with what I had to.

When I got around to Journey's block, I thought about calling her, until I saw all those buster-ass dudes sitting on the corner. I knew at least two of them had to be stick-up kids from the Ville, and although they all knew my father and Vince's crazy ass, that didn't always stop people from testing you.

Walking a straight line, I tried to avoid eye contact, but kept my head up at the same time to let them niggas know I wasn't scared. These were the same nut-ass dudes that tried to convince me to sell coke so I could get fly shit. The dumbest part about that was my dad made sure he kept me in the hottest, so that aspect confused me. Whatever. I just held my breath and counted to ten like I usually did, because that's how long it normally took me to get by.

"Look at this li'l nigga," the one they called Boom said to the crowd as I walked by. "Look like he got them new Jordans on."

"Yeah, it do, and I think I can fit them joints," another goon from the crowd said. I kept on walking like that shit ain't faze me, because neither one of their lame asses could touch me. I had my hand on my cell phone in my pocket, just in case I had to hit my dad up real quick. Truth be told, I knew none of them dudes had no real knuckle game, so this would be an easy win.

When I got up to the door, Journey was coming down the stairs, looking good as shit. My dick got hard instantly, but I promised her we would wait, so I tried to hold it down. For like four seconds, I thought about dipping back to Gina's to take her up on that offer later on tonight, but that chick was ran through, and I knew Journey was worth the wait.

"Damn, ma. Look at you," I said to her once she got outside. I held my hand out to help her down the steps, and I twirled her around in a circle to show her off to them markass dudes on the corner before I pulled her into a tight hug and kissed her on her lips. When I pulled back from her, it looked like she had been crying, and my smile turned into a look of concern instantly.

"What's wrong, baby? Did something happen?" I asked her as I locked eyes with her. I would lay down anybody who even thought about stepping to her. Journey was my world, and I swear I would put the lessons from the shooting range to good use out this bitch if somebody crossed her.

"No, I'm good, Khalid," she said unconvincingly, and I automatically took my vision to the corner, wondering who in the crowd I would have to take out.

"One of them niggas say something to you?" I asked her, mentally preparing myself for what I would have to do. There was too many of them then, but at three in the morning, it would be a different story.

"Naw, my uncle tripping again. That's all," she said while placing a smile on her face, I guess to make me feel better. I would handle her uncle, too, when the time came, but for now, I just wanted to enjoy the night.

"Did he put his hands on you?" I asked her, inspecting her body for any signs of abuse. I hated that she had to be around here by herself, but my mom wouldn't let me stay the night over here. I wanted to wrap her up in my arms and protect her from the world, but even little girls in the ghetto had to learn how to survive.

"No, baby, I'm good. Let's go to the movies," she said with another unconvincing smile. I decided to let it be what it was until she was ready to talk to me.

"Okay, baby, let's be out. You looking real good in that dress, too," I said to her as I hugged her from behind and pressed my erection against her butt. I slid my hands down her sides, realizing she had a thong on. She turned around and smiled at me with a devilish look on her face, and on some real shit, I was ready to skip the movie and go on upstairs.

"Come on, let's go," she said, taking my hand and pulling me behind her. I was ready to get it in, but I could wait.

When we got near the corner, I hugged Journey next to me a little tighter and eyeballed all those niggas, letting them see the dime I had on my arm. The look I gave them let them know they wouldn't be able to get in sniffing distance of my baby. After getting money from my dad, we hopped on the 36 trolley heading toward Fortieth Street. Everybody was checking my baby out, and I just smiled because I knew every dude that looked at her wished they had her. We were going to be together forever, regardless of any situation.

Bunz B

Now or Never

"Move in silence," I mouthed to the crew as we approached the store. The women inside were too busy conversing to pay any attention to us, and that's normally how shit went down.

Gary's simple-ass was staggering a little bit because he was so high, and I knew at that very moment that if shit went down, he would be the fall guy. I was a little disappointed in him, though, because he knew how important this was to the crew, and he was acting as the weakest link as usual. It made me wonder why I ever chose him to be my right hand man in the first place.

As I signaled to Jamel and Kev, they moved as planned and kicked in the door, startling the women on the other side as we rushed in. Gary had one woman at gunpoint. I assumed she was the owner because she was behind the counter. From my viewpoint, I could see that she was standing near some stairs that led down to a basement. The other woman was cowering in the corner under Kev's watchful eye, and all I had to do was grab the money and make a dash before one of the brothers came back to check on these ladies. I timed it perfectly, and if everything went as planned, we would be long gone before anyone showed up.

Watching everyone in the room, I jumped behind the counter and popped open the cash register, disappointed to see only a couple hundred dollars inside. That wouldn't put a dent in what I needed, but it was a start. Feeling around for a trap door or something of the sort, I came across a panel in the wall that revealed a safe once it was pulled back. "Yo, bitch, what's the combination?" I yelled to the woman that Gary had under his gun, hoping like hell she would cooperate. I would hate to have to spaz out on this bitch, but it would definitely go down if need be. I didn't need that kind of heat on me right at this moment. I just wanted to get this cash and get ghost.

She looked like she had possibly swallowed her tongue, but I needed answers now. Frustrated, I walked up to her and grabbed her by her throat, lifting her an inch off the floor and pinning her against the wall. She was shook beyond reason, and I just got even more pissed when I looked down and saw that piss had splashed against my shoes from her going on herself. I was ready to gut-punch her ass, because I just got these joints.

"I said, what's the combination?" I spoke to her with my face mere inches from hers. I placed her back on the floor so that she could breathe. She took a few deep breaths before spitting out the code.

I signaled Gary to hold me down while I went to pop the safe, hoping for her sake that was the right code. The first time, it didn't work, and I was about to turn around and blast her simple ass, but I tried it again, and this time it popped right open.

"Jackpot!" I said more to myself than anyone else as I unloaded the neatly stacked bundles of money and coke that went deep into the safe. I knew it had to easily have been twenty thousand in cash in this joint, and that was a good start. I had my eye on another store that I was sure had cash flow in there too, and that would be enough for me to get my money up and hide out for a while until shit died down. Once I had all the money gathered, I stood up, signaling for my crew to kill the witnesses so that we could roll out. We couldn't just run out of the store, though, because we didn't know who was outside, and we didn't want to look suspect when we left.

Kev didn't hesitate to pull the trigger, the silencer making it possible to kill in silence and not alert the neighbors. When I looked over at Gary's simple ass, he was looking like he didn't want to do it, and was on some real high shit. I swear I always had to do shit myself.

"Yo, off that bitch," I said to him in a normal tone, so as not to get loud in this place. This nigga was still hesitating. Fed up with the situation, I moved to kill the woman myself, but before I could reach them, he knocked her down the steps where she hit a washing machine with a hard thud. I thought about shooting down the steps to make sure she was a goner, but my gun didn't have a silencer on it, and I liked to kill close up so that I could see the fear in a person's eyes. She wasn't moving, though, so I figured she was as good as dead. We only had a few minutes to get in and get out, so going down the stairs would take too much time anyway.

Giving Gary one last disappointed look, I signaled for us to file out, and we did just that, stepping over the bloody mess that was the other woman, being careful not to step in the crimson puddle that had formed around her body that would leave possible footprints.

Once back in the car, we didn't say a word to each other, making our way back to the hood as quickly as possible with out drawing attention to ourselves. I still had that body in the back that we needed to ditch, because I could smell it on the inside of the car now, and it had been in there for three days, so it was time. I almost felt bad when I saw the young boy's mom on the news, crying because she hadn't seen her son in a week, but he owed me money, so I had to do what I had to do. He threatened to snitch me out to the feds because they were looking for both of our asses, and I couldn't have that shit over my head.

Not paying attention, I rolled through a red light, kicking myself for not slowing down in time to stop at the light. I thought I was cool, until I saw the law turn the corner behind me and flash his lights. I knew I couldn't stop because we had the body and the heat in the car, along with the bag of money we just got from the store. We were ass out anyway, because the car had stolen tags on it, and the license plate didn't match the vehicle we were in.

Taking a glance around the car, everyone was cool but alert, except for Gary's simple ass. He was knocked the fuck out in the corner, because he was high off them damn pills. He would be taking the loss for this tonight and we all knew it.

I sped up a little faster, and the cop car did the same, following me through five or six more lights. We had to act fast before he called in back-up and they were able to catch up to us. I wasn't going to jail tonight, and Jamel and Kev had the same plan I had.

"Yo, I'm going through this next light then I'm coming to a dead stop. That'll be your opportunity to jet or get caught," I said as I grabbed the duffle bag and pulled the strap over my head so that it could wrap around my body. I felt bad for Gary for a split second, because he was one of the best I had. He just couldn't leave that shit alone. They all got ready, tucking the guns under the seats and wiping fingerprints from the door-knobs and dash. I had on gloves, so I wasn't worrying about anything but getting away. We all knew what to do and where to meet, so I moved a little faster, causing the cop car to do the same.

Once I crossed the light, I slammed on the brakes, throwing the car in park and popping the door open, hauling ass down the street and cutting through the alley. The cops knew that once we got in the projects it would be a wrap, because once in a building, who's to say we didn't just go out the back or dipped off in one of the apartments?

Toya already knew I was coming there after the robbery, so I headed her way. The cop didn't know whether to run after us or stay at the car, because we all spread out. He couldn't chase all three of us at the same time, but I left him a little gift in the car, and I would make sure I hit Gary up once he was booked.

I could hear sirens coming from everywhere, so when I got to the projects, I slowed down and walked at a regular pace to blend in with the crowd, so that I wouldn't look obvious. I spoke to a few people on the walk by as I entered on Fifty-fourth Street, stopping at the deli to get a strawberry White Owl and a double deuce of Heineken, opting to pull money out of my pocket instead of the duffle bag.

As planned, Toya had her door unlocked, so I just walked in and sat down on the couch, chilling out until she was done doing the woman's hair in the kitchen. I was pissed because I told her to have an empty house when I got there, but bitches never listened, so what was I supposed to do? So that the women in the kitchen wouldn't recognize me if they flashed my grill on the news, I went into the bedroom and stretched out on the bed until she was done. Toya would be mad because I had dirty clothes on her white comforter, but I had enough to buy her a million comforter sets, and by the time I got finished knocking the bottom out that pussy, she wouldn't be mad anymore, so I wasn't too worried about it.

I wanted to turn on the television to see how it all went down with Gary, but I didn't want to know this soon. His simple ass made me sick. I should have just offed him myself to save time. I didn't think he would snitch or anything like that, but he was useless unless he got his shit together, and I doubted he ever would.

A half hour later, Toya came in to the room, pissed that I was lying on top of her comforter with my boots still on. I got up and hopped in the shower to shut her ass up, plus I still had the young girl on me from earlier today, so I had to wash her shit off me too. By the time I came out, Toya had the television on with a breaking story from the cops, saying how they were looking for three suspects in a police chase and possible robbery, and that they had caught one guy because he was asleep in the back of the getaway car.

They didn't have a clear picture of us from the dashboard camera of the cop car. All I saw was three men dressed in all black, so we'd be cool for a while. Her eyes got big when they said they found a body in the trunk, as well as guns and drugs in the vehicle, at the time they pulled the car over.

"Who got left in the car?" she asked, a stunned look on her face. I didn't even bother to answer, because all that shit would be coming out over the next couple of days anyway. Instead of answering her, I turned the TV off, pulled her ass to the edge of the bed, and tore the pussy up to put her to sleep. I personally couldn't sleep myself, and I really didn't want to turn the television on, so I laid there in the dark, staring at the ceiling and contemplating my next move. I would lay low here for a while. As long as I fed Toya's pockets, she'd be cool, but I knew I would have to move out before they found out who we were and the hood got hot. I would break the money down tomorrow so that I could give Kev and Jamel their cuts, and I would give Gary's cut to his people, because they would be needing it for a lawyer. I just hoped he learned his lesson this time and left that shit alone. Things were about to get hectic, though. I just wasn't sure if I was ready to deal with the bullshit yet.

Shanyce Davidson

Caught Out There

"I'm not fucking with that shit like that, and I don't know why that much money is missing, Joey," I said to my son's father while trying to muster up an innocent look.

I fucked up again, but I swear I was not hooked on that shit. This time I'd used most of the money to buy a pocketbook, and I spent the rest on some Snow White that I copped from Journey on the low. I begged her not to tell Khalid, or anyone for that matter, what was up, but maybe she did. How else would Joey know I was getting high?

"Shanyce, I know how much money I had, and a thousand dollars is missing from the stash. You look fuckin' high, and I heard you be coppin' from up West Philly. I ain't got time for this shit." "But Joey—"

"Shut the fuck up, Shanyce. Khalid will be staying at Journey's house until further notice.

Get your shit together or we'll never be back. I shouldn't have to hide shit from you because I can't trust your simple ass. I ain't fuckin' with no fiend."

What could I say? I knew Joey would get tired of me sooner or later, but to the point where he would take my son from me? I didn't think it would ever get that serious— and I was not a fiend. A fiend sucks dick for product when they can't scrape up the change to buy it. I, on the other hand, had the money to buy it, even if it was borrowed from Joey. I say borrowed because I planned to put it back; he just found out before I could.

I was standing in the doorway of my son's room while Joey went through his things to pack him a bag. You would think that I would have been more concerned, but my mind kept wandering to that small bag of powder I had tucked in the corner of my purse. A part of me wanted Joey to stay so we could work it out, but a small part of me wanted him to leave so I could sit in my room and get my head on right. I could stop whenever I wanted to, though; I wasn't worried about that. I just didn't need this nigga riding my head right now.

On the low, I saw Joey tuck a gun inside of the duffle bag he was filling with my boy's clothes, and it made me wonder what else he was stashing in Khalid's room. And did Khalid know? Or was that gun even in Khalid's room to begin with? I would just wait for Joey to leave to do a thorough investigation. Right now I had to make sense of this situation. Khalid was getting so big now, and I would hate for him to have to worry about me when he should be concentrating on school. Journey was such a nice girl, too, and I was glad to see that they were still close. Journey didn't look like the type that was fucking yet, so I wasn't really worried. Besides, if they did decide to take the plunge, I taught him everything he needed to know about protecting himself. I was too damn fine, and too damn young, to be a grandmother. I didn't even realize I was drifting in and out until Joey brushed past me to get out of the room and almost knocked me down. I loved Joey so much, and I knew what I had to do to get shit back tight. He had always been a good provider for me and Khalid, and I could always depend on him to hold me down. I would fix things between us. I just needed to get this hit up in me first.

By the time I got downstairs, Joey was just closing and locking the door, so I took that opportunity to chill out on the couch and get comfortable. He wouldn't be back for a while, so I could do what I needed to do right there and it would be cleaned up before he got home. I didn't want to have to get back up for anything, so before I pulled anything out of my pocketbook, I went to the kitchen and made me a quick grub, so that I could fall back.

Clicking on the television and putting my food to the side, I pulled out my works from my pocketbook and spread everything out on the coffee table. I'd grabbed a fresh syringe from the job, so I was straight. My hands were almost shaking from the anticipation.

Holding the small vial of Snow White up to my nose, I sniffed it through the plastic before I broke the seal and tapped half of its contents out onto a metal spoon. My mouth started to water in anticipation as I dropped a capful of water onto the spoon and stirred it up a bit before placing the flame from my lighter under it. My eyes glazed over as the solution began to bubble, and I carefully placed a piece of a cotton ball on top to soak up the excess before pulling it up into the syringe.

Gently placing the filled syringe on the table after tapping the excess air out, I pulled my Gucci belt from the loops in my jeans in one quick motion, because I left the tourniquet I normally used at the job. Quickly wrapping the belt around my thigh, I pulled it as tight as I could, until I could see a good vein bulge in the spot in the back of my knee. I rotated legs so that it wasn't obvious, but I knew I would have to get a better spot soon.

My hands began to shake more as I secured the belt through a punctured hole. I grabbed the syringe from the table, preparing myself for the best feeling in life.

I thought I heard keys at the door, but I chalked it up to paranoia, because I was scared that Joey would bust in. Steadying my hand, I positioned the syringe and brought it closer to my vein, ready for ecstasy. At the moment the needle punctured my skin and I begin to release the drug into my system, I looked up to see Joey standing in the doorway. I wanted to pull the needle out, but my thumb was still pressing down in a slow motion on the top of the syringe, and I couldn't stop it. At one point, I thought I saw two Joeys standing there, but I could only focus long enough to put the syringe back on the table and wipe my nose on the back of my hand. I knew my speech would be slurred, but I tried to talk to him anyway.

"What you doin' back here so soon?" I thought I said, as the effect of the drugs made my body feel heavy. All I could do was lean back on the couch and try to keep my head from slumping, but I was already losing the battle. This shit that Journey gave me must not have been cut all the way, because I never felt like this before. Damn, I only used half the cap. A whole one probably would have killed my ass.

I couldn't hear him talking over my heartbeat, but I knew he was, because through the slits of my eyes, I could see his mouth moving. He was yelling something in my face, and I was trying to at least look like I was interested in what he was saying, but I don't think I was pulling it off well.

Closing my eyes one last time, I tried to take a deep breath so that I could get back into the game, but out of nowhere, it felt like I got hit in my eye with a ton of bricks as a bright light flashed before me. With my one good eye left, I could see Joey's fist balled up and him coming in for another blow. I got up what strength I could to shield my face, but it felt like I was being held down, and my body started to itch all over like I had the chicken pox or something. I wanted to scream, but all I could taste was blood from the busted lip I now had, and it felt like I might be spitting out a tooth or three before this was all over.

Joey lost his damn mind up in here, beating on me like I was a stranger. I began to cry, thinking that would stop him, but it felt like he hit me harder. My tears burned my face. It felt like he was leaving fist prints all over my body. He killed my only brother years ago, even though he would never admit it, so I had no one to call to retaliate for me. I was dead wrong, though, so I just laid there and took the beating until I passed out.

I didn't think I was out that long, but when I woke up, the house was pitch black. I felt like I had gotten hit by a train. I couldn't open my left eye, and it gave me a headache just thinking about how I got it. It took me a minute, but I was finally able to get up off the couch and flick the light on, and that alone almost made me hit the floor.

Everything was gone. The TV, my pocketbook, and my get-high—everything was gone. I turned and saw that the door was cracked open a little, and came to the conclusion that someone must have come in after Joey left, but who? Everyone knew who my man was. Would they really blatantly disrespect him like that? I wanted to call him and tell him what happened, but he just beat the shit out of me, so what difference would it make to him?

Locking the door and securing it with the dead bolt, I went upstairs to get what was left of my stash so that I could get it together. It was only a little bit left, and I wouldn't buy anymore after this, so I would be straight. I needed to get my family back; there was nothing else I had to live for.

Pulling my stash from out of my Gucci knee boot tucked way back in the closet, I sat down on the edge of the bed and chopped the shit up with a razor on my compact mirror. I would have really rather shot the shit up, but whoever came in there took my shit, so that didn't leave me too many options. I never snorted before, but my logic was it couldn't be any worse than shooting the shit, so I went for it.

The shit burned the hell out of my nose, and my eyes watered up immediately. I felt light-headed, so I lay back on the bed, hoping the room would stop spinning soon and I didn't overdose.

Thinking back to when I first met Joey, tears streamed down my face. They were burning the shut eye like I had poured salt inside, but I couldn't stop. Joey and Khalid were all I had, but I didn't know if they would be enough to keep me from wanting the feeling I got from this Snow White. I mean, you only live once, right? Now was my time, but I wasn't going to get caught up in this shit. I could stop whenever I was ready. That was my story, and I was sticking to it.

Journey Clayton

My Last First Kiss

We held hands as we walked from the trolley tunnel at Nineteenth and Market, over a block to Chestnut Street, because the movie we wanted to see wasn't playing in University City. Khalid kept whispering in my ear, telling me how good I looked, and I was blushing all over the place and giggling like a young girl. I was so wet and anxious to give my virginity to Khalid that I couldn't wait to get home. On the real, I wanted to skip the movie and all that, but Khalid liked coming down here, because we could walk down to the arcade on Fifteenth Street afterwards and chill in there for a while before we went home. Our favorite game was House of the Dead, and the last time we played, we almost ended it.

Between boards, he would lean over and kiss me, and that was turning me on even more. On the flip side, I had so many secrets I wanted to tell him. I just didn't know how. I wanted to tell him that his mom came to me a few times to cop, and even though I was not supposed to be selling drugs, just bagging it up, I gave it to her because I thought Vince sent her around for it. On some real shit, did I want to know that my mom and dad were on that shit? Maybe, because I found out when it was too late, and now I was parent-less.

"What you thinking about?" Khalid asked me as he hugged me closer to him. We were now leaned up against the wall outside the arcade, contemplating getting a slice from Spiro's Pizza before we hopped on the trolley to get back down the way. He was really dragging this shit out, be-cause I was ready to give him the business right now.

"You and me. I have a gift for you," I said to him before I tongue-kissed him until we were both out of breath. We smiled at each other afterwards, and I was glad that he walked right past the pizza shop and went directly to the trolley stop on Fifteenth Street. I was ready to get things poppin', and since I knew he wasn't expecting me to break him off, it would be even better.

The trolley ride seemed much longer tonight than normal, but the 36 was right there. We just had to wait about ten minutes before it pulled off. We walked from the movies to the trolley, and at this time of night, most of the trolleys waited until they were almost full to pull off. I didn't know if they got there too early or were just starting out or what, but that's the way it went. All the trolleys that ran in the city stopped at Fifteenth Street; you just had to wait for your number trolley to pull up.

We sat all the way in the back of the empty trolley. I couldn't wait to get home. I was afraid, because all I really knew and felt about sex were the horrible things that my uncle did to me. I knew with Khalid it wouldn't be the same, but I couldn't really pinpoint what would be different about it besides the fact that it wouldn't be forced. I was on fire, and wished for a few seconds that the driver would skip all the stops until we got to ours.

Khalid got off the trolley first to make sure there were no cars trying to speed around the trolley, as if they didn't know people would be getting off. He held my hand all the way down the block. When we got near Choice's crib, I could see Vince eyeballing me from the porch. I acted straight like I ain't see his ass on the walk by. He promised me when I was nine that when I turned fourteen he would be the first to bust my cherry, and that's why it was so important for me to give it to Khalid tonight. I wouldn't give Vince the satisfaction.

Those same guys that were outside when we left were still standing on the corner when we approached the block. They hated Khalid because he scooped me and I wouldn't give anyone else the time of day, but them fucking with him wouldn't make me want them more. Guys can be so stupid at times, I swear. I could feel Khalid tense up a little, so I squeezed his hand to assure him he had nothing to worry about.

"Yo, I would bend that ass right over. I know that pussy is tight," one of the guys said when we crossed the street. Khalid simply smiled and kissed me on the lips in front of them before looking back and ushering me up the steps. I would have to talk to him about that later, because feeding into their nonsense could cause problems down the line, and I wasn't in the mood.

When we got upstairs, I made him wait in the living room so that I could double check that my bedroom was in place for him and that Vince hadn't gone through my stuff. I had to dig through about nine pocketbooks before I found the condoms I got from CVS a while ago, hoping I wouldn't have to give one to Vince before

Khalid. We had the same sex education class last year, so we made sure to pay extra attention and ask any questions to the teacher before school was let out. It seemed kind of odd, because it seemed like everyone was already having sex and we were behind the times, but to me, that just made it more special because I wasn't just giving up the booty to just anyone. I was so in love with Khalid, I wouldn't have this any other way.

He was sitting on the couch when I came out, and was looking real good to me. I made sure the door was locked, sliding over the dead bolt so that Vince couldn't just walk in on us. I grabbed his hand and walked him into the bedroom. He looked different in the semi-light room, the only light source being a strawberry Glade candle I had burning on the dresser. His smile matched mine as he sat down on the bed, and I used the remote to hit play on my little pink stereo in the corner. I made up a slow jams tape with about twelve songs that I knew would set the mood right. Every time I heard these songs, they made me think of making love to Khalid, and I hoped he felt the same way.

I was a little nervous when I walked up to him and stood between his legs. He had a gentle touch, and wasn't all fumbling like I thought he would be. We promised that we would wait for each other, and it crossed my mind for four seconds that he might have gotten it already, because Lord knows everyone in the damn school was on his dick. Pushing the thought from my mind, I concentrated on the good feelings I got from his hands rubbing up and down my body. He sucked on my hard nipples through the material of my dress. It created a cool sensation when he took his mouth off and latched on to the other one. His fingers did a slow dance across my clit at the same time, causing my knees to buckle a little from the sensation. With my eyes closed and my head thrown back, I allowed Khalid to fondle me until I felt like I was going to explode.

My uncle never made me feel like this, and my head was spinning, because I didn't know whether to stop him or let him continue. Vince made me feel so dirty, and I tried to hide my body from him. Khalid made me feel loved, and I felt like I loved him even more. "Khalid, I feel like I'm about to—"

"Shhh," he said to me before I could finish my sentence. Standing up, he pulled my dress over my head, afterward laying me on the bed so that he could remove my thong. He wanted me to keep my shoes on, so I obliged, not really understanding why. I had a towel laid out on the bed, because I was expecting to bleed a little, and I didn't want to mess up my sheets.

"You nervous, baby?" Khalid asked me as I felt his now naked body next to mine on my bed. His hardness rested on my thigh, and I could feel it pulsate in tune with our breathing. He was big to be such a young boy, and for the first time that night, I was really scared to do it.

"Yeah, a little," I admitted to him. I was scared a lot, but I couldn't let Vince have the satisfaction of stealing my innocence. Khalid was the love of my life, and he deserved it.

"Don't be. I was watching this movie the other day, and it looked fairly easy. We'll just take our time, and if it hurts too bad, I'll stop, okay?"

"Okay."

I was nervous, but we were able to talk each other through it, and it turned out perfect. Khalid was ready to just dip in my honey pot, but I had to show him what I learned about foreplay from the romance books I was allowed to read. We did a lot of rubbing and caressing each other, and it didn't take much to convince him to go down on me to get me wetter than I was. I didn't think I would be able to orgasm from insertion, so I at least wanted to before the night was out.

Khalid did a good job with orally satisfying me, paying attention to what I told him to do. Part of it was from the books I'd read, but most of it was from the feeling I got when Vince went

down on me. I had him mimic what Vince did,
and it felt so good. A part of me felt horrible
because I knew I wasn't supposed to like what
Vince did to me, but the response my body gave
from his touch was uncontrollable. I wanted to
hate it but I couldn't.

I surprised him by returning the favor, and he
exploded in a short minute. I did what I had to
do to get him back up so that we could do what
we came here for.

"You ready to do this?" I asked him as I ca-
ressed his hard dick in between my thighs. I
could feel it thumping against my clit, and I
couldn't wait to finally feel him inside of me.
"Are you?" he asked, sounding more nervous
than I was.

"Yeah."

He lay back on the bed, and I used both my
hands to roll the condom down on him before we
got started. He looked unsure as he rested himself in between my legs, asking me if I was sure
once more before he started to put it in. "Okay,
ma. I'm going to push it in slow." He started to
push himself inside of me, and my body tensed
at the pressure I felt down there. I broke out into
a sweat, and almost couldn't breathe as he tried
to work himself inside of me. He continued to
kiss me softly all over my face and rubbed up

and down my sides as he slowed grinded me to get himself in. A tear escaped my closed eyes and ran down the side of my face because it hurt so bad. It felt like I was full, but he seemed to have more to go.

"Damn, girl, you feel so good," he moaned in my ear as he continued to push and pull until he was all the way inside of me. I wanted to scream because the burning and pain was too much, but I just bit my lip and hoped it would get better soon.

It felt like he was finally all the way in me, and it began to get a little easier for him to go in and out. The pain slowly subsided, and it began to feel so good, as I was finally able to push back. I moaned in his ear and told him how much I loved him. He doing the same in return.

I couldn't even hear the radio anymore; all I could hear was our breathing and the sounds my pussy made every time he pushed in deep. I knew I wasn't ready for all the hardcore shit yet, but just thinking about doing it doggy style and riding him had me at an orgasm in no time.

Khalid held me tighter as he approached his orgasm, and I had to gently remind him to pull out before he came, just in case the condom broke. We couldn't afford for me to get pregnant, and even with a condom, you still could if there was a small hole in it.

My legs felt wobbly, and I couldn't move. The clock revealed that only about ten minutes had actually passed, but that was the longest ten minutes of my life. I got up from the bed to go wash up and put a pad on so that I wouldn't bleed all over the place. Khalid had to be home by two or his mom would have a fit, so I wanted to at least be able to chill with him before he had to roll out.

On the way out of the room, his phone began to ring, so I gave him some privacy while he talked to whoever it was. I didn't know how long I would be bleeding for, but I'd look it up on the Internet, because I wanted to do it again as soon as possible.

Looking in the mirror, I noticed a small passion mark on the side of my neck that I would have to cover up before Vince saw it. I was a woman now, and the thought made me smile. Finally I beat Vince at something, and there was no turning back now. It would be Khalid and me forever.

Khalid Street

King of the World

"Hello?" I spoke into the phone when I saw my dad's number pop up on the screen. I was nervous because I thought it was Gina calling me with her bullshit again, and I didn't want to have to explain to Journey how she got my number in the first place.

"Khalid, meet me on the steps. You'll be staying at the crib with Journey for a while. I already talked to Vince."

I was shocked into speechlessness. Did he say I would be staying with Journey for a while? Why didn't he take me to my grandmother's or my aunt's house? I know my dad didn't know me and Journey were intimate, but he had to know I was digging the hell out of her. Furthermore, I was surprised my mom even agreed to that. My dad hated my mom's family, and his family lived in Neshaminy, so I guess this was the closest spot until he could decide what to do next. My mom must have really pissed him off this time, and I couldn't believe that Vince went along with the plan. I had a bunch of questions, but the tone of his voice let me know that now wasn't the time to ask.

"Okay, Pop, I'll meet you out front." I got up and put my clothes back on, even my shoes, so that he wouldn't suspect we were in here doing anything that we shouldn't be. I told Journey to get completely dressed and sit in the living room, just in case he came upstairs to investigate shit. I didn't want to give him any reason to change his mind.

By the time I got outside, my dad was walking up the block with my duffle bag, packed to capacity, swung over his shoulder. I didn't think I would be staying that long, but who was I to argue with a decision he made? He would let me know when it was time for me to go.

"Listen, I got some heat in this bag. Hide it for me when you get upstairs, and don't let anybody know you have it. I'll come back for it later," my dad said to me while checking his surroundings. I wondered why he didn't just hide it himself, but knew better than to ask. I wasn't even sure why he needed it hidden in the first place, but that's what he wanted, so that's what it would be.

"What about Mom? Is she okay?" I asked, wondering why she hadn't bothered to call me all day. My mom was usually on my heels, but lately she'd been acting weird, and I just couldn't put my finger on it.

"Your mom is going through something right now," he said to me while looking the other way. That usually meant he was trying to sugar coat something, but he would usually keep it real with me later, so I would just wait. "Everything is cool, though. Don't go to the house. Just chill around here until I tell you it's cool to go back home."

I decided not to push the issue just yet. Depending on how long I would be staying here, that would determine my investigation. He peeled off four hundred dollars from the knot in his pocket, and we talked for a little while longer before he gave me a pound and we parted ways.

"Remember what I told you to do," he said to me, reminding me to hide the gun when I got upstairs.

I sprinted up the steps into the house, finding Journey sitting on the couch, looking like an angel. No one would have thought that we were just doing the nasty grown-up, and I wanted to keep things that way. I set my bag in her room before taking a seat next to her on the couch.

"Who was that?" she asked me as I sat down and pulled her into my arms.

"My dad packed me an overnight bag. He said Vince said I can stay here for a while, but I'm concerned about my mom." I spoke honestly to her, not sure if I should disobey my dad and go around there anyway, or just stay put and let whatever happened happen.

"I'm sure he has a good reason, so let's just chill and finish our date," she said as she stood up and pulled me with her.

Journey took the time to lock the door and shut off all the lights before we went back to her room. I stripped down to my boxers and climbed in the bed. She followed behind me with only her panties on. I couldn't believe she finally let me get it. I was glad her back was to me so that she couldn't see me smiling all hard and shit, and I was suddenly glad I had made the decision to not get with Gina and wait on my baby girl. She cuddled up next to me in a spooning position and I rubbed her belly while she lay in my arms. I knew we were going to have a pretty baby one of these days, and I was looking forward to spending the rest of my life with her. "You okay, ma?"

"Yeah, I'm good. I'm bleeding a little, though," she responded, snuggling up closer to me.

"That's natural, babe. You'll be fine by tomorrow."

"Somebody paid attention in sex education, huh?" she said jokingly, both of us laughing out loud.

"Yeah, I guess I did."

I was in the midst of dozing off, not paying too much attention to the television. I would get up during the night to hide that burner for my dad once Journey was asleep. I just had a nagging feeling telling me to go around the crib, but I couldn't drag Journey out in the street this late at night.

I was finally able to fall asleep around one. Journey had been asleep way before that, and it felt good lying next to my baby. I was having a horrible dream, though, that a guy was chasing me. I had blood all over my shirt, but I didn't know if it was his or mine. I had my dad's gun in my hand, and just as I decided to turn around and shoot, I heard a loud bang on the front door.

Both of us jumped up and looked at each other, thinking it might be Vince at the door. Journey got out of the bed and threw on a nightshirt and grabbed a blanket from the bed so it would look like I was asleep in the living room. I lay down on the couch and let Journey answer the door so that if it was Vince, he wouldn't snap out on me. The banging was insistent, and we were both scared to death at who could be on the other side.

"Who is it?" Journey asked while trying to make out the image on the other side of the peephole.

"It's me, Shanyce. Khalid's mom. I need you to hook me up again, baby girl. Vince said it was cool."

Journey's entire body went rigid, and the look on my face was of confusion. What did she mean she needed another hook-up? I knew Journey cooked and bagged up product for her uncle sometimes, but was she selling that shit to my mother? Was my mother turned out on Snow White?

"Open the door, Journey," I said to her, now standing up from the couch. I needed to see with my own eyes that the woman on the other side of the door was really my mom and not some imposter.

She hesitated, but eventually cast her eyes to the floor and opened the door. My breath was taken away as I laid my eyes upon my mother's disheveled form. Tears sprung up in my eyes instantly, but I had to hold it down.

"Mom, who did this to you? Who did this?" I asked as I walked her to the kitchen table to sit her down. Journey turned the light on and stood in the doorway, looking like she was scared to get any closer.

"It's nothing. Me and your dad got in a fight, that's all. What are you doing here?" she asked as she slumped against the table. I couldn't believe that shit I was seeing, and Journey was still cowering in the doorway like she was scared I was going to spaz out.

I didn't answer. I pulled Journey into the living room instead to see what the hell my mom was doing coming here for drugs, and how many times she'd been there before. I knew the love of my life was not selling my mother product and I wasn't aware of it.

"Journey, your answer better be a good one."

"Khalid, it's not my fault," she began as tears started streaming down her face. "Your mom came here one night and told me that Vince sent her here, so I gave her what she asked for. I didn't find out until later on that she was telling a lie."

"And why didn't you tell me?"

"Because your dad told me not to."

At that moment, my world came tumbling down around me. I didn't know whether to go left or right, and I was ready to take that gun my dad gave me and kill his ass with it. Since when did we start keeping secrets? I started pulling on my clothes so that I could get up out of there. I felt like I was suffocating.

"Where are you going?" Journey said as she tried to block me from leaving the room. I picked her up by her waist and moved her to the side. She followed behind me like a puppy dog. She was crying hysterically by now, but I had another mission.

"Come on, Mom. Let's go," I said to her as I helped her out of the chair.

"I'm not going nowhere without some Snow White. Vince said I could have it," she responded as she fought me to get up from the chair.

Journey looked helpless, but I couldn't deal with her right now. I had to get my mom home and in bed, and then I had to go get at my dad. My mom fought me tooth and nail, but I finally got her out of the house and down the steps. Those same hustle boys were on the corner, and I wished for a second that I had brought that gun out with me.

My mom took me through it all the way back to the crib, and on the walk by, I saw Vince sitting on Choice's porch, but I couldn't even stop. He had a smirk on his face that made my skin boil, and I added him to the list too. Somebody was going to pay for this, and if I had to start at the top until I found out who it was, that's the way it would be.

Bunz B

Shiesty Shit

I'd told Toya on more than one occasion not to be having them nappy-headed bitches up in here, but she insisted that she had money to make, even though I was breaking her off. I didn't want anyone to know I was here, and that shit pissed me off, because Lord forbid I had to take a piss or something. I couldn't even go out of the room if she had somebody out there.

I'd been knee-deep in the news, though, and the law had a bid on my head like crazy. A hundred thousand for whoever could find my black ass. That's why I had to keep Toya on lock, because she would definitely say some shit just for the money. Word on the street was that Gary was so fucked up when the cops got him that he was in jail for three days before he woke up and realized where he was. They just left him to rot in the cell. A dead man can't testify in court, so they would have woke him up eventually, but I told him so many times to stop fucking with that pancakes and syrup. That shit be having you on tilt, and now he saw where the shit got him.

Chancing a walk by in the living room, I saw that Toya was doing the little young girl's hair. Vince's niece, Journey. She was in there crying the blues because her and her boyfriend must have been about to break up. I was wondering who was hitting that shit, because shorty had it going on.

Her profile was the truth. She filled out what looked to be a nice D cup, and mami had hips. I could tell her ass was big just from the side view. That shit made me hard just looking at it, and I knew for certain I had to find a way to get at that. Vince didn't really fuck with me like that, but I knew if I came at him about moving these bricks of coke I had from the spot we just hit, he'd do business. Even though Joey wanted to strike me out of the equation, Vince's greedy-for-money ass would deal with me on the low if he could come up off it. He'd done so in the past, so he would probably do it again. Then I could see how to get next to her.

I was ear-hustling hard as shit, and from what I could gather, she was fucking with Joey's son. I'd been meaning to get at that nigga for a minute. We still had beef over that bullshit robbery we did back in the day, and I knew push come to shove, I would have to lay him down before he came at me. He'd tried so many times, but I stayed off the radar for that particular reason. He almost caught me slipping one night at the deli, but I grabbed one of the young girls in the store so that I could get out. I knew Joey would never shoot an innocent bystander on purpose.

At any rate, I didn't know too much about Khalid, so I'd have to send my boys to test him and see what he was about. It sounded like they had a petty argument; I just had to see if he was really ready to give shorty up. He was throwing her to the wolves, and I'd be right there to catch her ass.

I watched her from the cut while they were talking, and Toya was giving her advice that she should have been using her damn self. How the fuck was she gonna tell the young girl how to draw her man back in when she was single as the day is long? Did that shit work for her? I just laughed to myself as I went and lay back across the bed.

I had the television turned to a porn flick joint, and I had the volume down, because I didn't want Toya spazzing out with the young girl here. Although I was watching the movie, I was picturing Journey in here giving me the business. I had my dick out, stroking it until it felt like it couldn't get any harder. I briefly thought about tagging both their asses at the same time, but I knew they wouldn't go for that shit.

"Ay, Toya," I called into the kitchen. She came and peeked her head in the doorway, looking like I was irritating her and shit.

"What is it, B? I'm almost done with her hair."

"Suck my dick real fast," I said while still stroking myself. She looked at me like I was crazy, and instead of responding, she slammed the bedroom door shut. I could hear her saying some shit to Journey as she walked back to the kitchen, and I just shook my head.

Flicking the station to the news, I went from having a rock hard dick to limp when I saw Jamel being led out in handcuffs from the building right next to mine. Turning the volume up, I leaned forward to hear what he had to say. I knew he was mad because I had yet to break down the cash from the robbery, and I had my cell phone turned off since I got here, so I hadn't talked to anyone. Yeah, I was wrong, but that's what the simple ass got for letting me jet with the cash.

"I bet if you check the projects, you'll find who you lookin' for, playa," Jamel said into the camera as they led him to the car. He didn't try to hide his face or anything like that. Most criminals be tryin'a hide under a hooded sweat shirt or something, but he took his shit like a man and walked with his head up. He just sent the wolves after me, though, so I'd definitely have to get at him about it later.

Grabbing Toya's house phone off the nightstand, I called my cell phone to check my messages, and the voice informed me that my mailbox was full. I had several messages from Jamel and Kev, threatening to kill me when they found me, because no one knew where I was hiding out. I had a feeling one, if not both of these dudes was going to dime me out, so I had to set some shit in motion quick.

Toya came back into the room looking like she didn't feel like getting into nothing with me. I was cool with that, because I had another plan for her anyway. She was about to earn her keep, and not with her dry-ass pussy.

"Yo, you and the boy Vince is cool, right?" I asked her as I started pulling the bricks of coke out of my duffle bag.

"Yeah, we okay. I haven't been able to holler at him since you been here, though. Why? What, you about to leave?" "No, bitch, I'm not. And I been paying my way here, so go ahead with that bullshit. This is what I need you to do . . ."

I knew Vince and them didn't fuck with me like that, but by the time I got what I needed from them, I would be sitting up in Miami or some shit, living the good life. I'd hate to have to murk Toya after all this, so I hoped she played her cards right. There wasn't room for any mistakes.

Shanyce Davidson

Stuck on Tilt

I was not expecting my son to answer the door when I got there. I knew he wasn't home, but I thought maybe Joey took him to his family's house or some shit. And poor Journey, I knew she was fit to be tied right now. I just needed one last hit and I'd be cool, but Khalid looked like he was falling apart at the seams. He had to grow up eventually; I just hated that it had to be like this.

I needed some money. Maybe I could take one of my pocketbooks back to the store. I couldn't find my car keys, but I didn't think Joey took the keys from me. I could ask him to take me down there, but I didn't feel like arguing with him right now. Besides, I done tore the house up looking for his stash, so I had to put shit back in order before he popped back up. If I could get myself together, maybe I could work a deal out with him to get a hit. I'd go into a program; I just needed this one last high before I called it a day.

Khalid had been lurking around me since he got here. His poor eyes were bloodshot, and every time I walked past him, he just looked the other way. How was I supposed to explain to him that I got caught out there? His dad had the shit around me all the time, and even back in the day, both Joey and me used to get down. I guess Joey was stronger than I was.

I was getting that antsy, feeling like it's bugs crawling on my skin, and I can't keep still. I just needed one small rock and I'd be in there. For a second I thought I saw a rock on the floor, but it turned out to be an earring back from a piece of jewelry I had. I didn't want to go there, but I did have some nice pieces I could pawn. Then I could go see my boy down the bottom.

"Khalid, are you upset with Journey?" I asked my son when I finally got the courage to face him in the living room. It looked like he had straightened up a little. I'd been kind of letting the place go lately, so he did what he could.

"That's my business, Ma. Just go upstairs and rest." I looked at my son, and it was like I was seeing him for the first time. He'd grown up to be quite handsome. I'd never seen him hurt like this. The thing is, there was nothing I could do to make it better.

"Journey didn't know, Khalid. I told her a lie to get the drugs. It wasn't her fault, and I didn't know you were there."

"Ma, I don't want to talk about it. Just go upstairs and rest."

There was nothing more to say. I had officially disappointed my son. I turned to go upstairs, but instead of going to my room, I went to Khalid's instead. He had definitely grown over the years. His walls, which were once adorned with posters of his favorite cartoon characters, were now covered with posters of Beyoncé, 50 Cent, and various other music artists. He had a cute picture of him and Journey sitting on one nightstand, and a photo of me and his dad on the dresser.

I didn't know where to look at first, and then I remembered Joey taking stuff out of the closet. First look revealed a normal closet, but I knew enough to know Joey was smarter than that. I felt around on the sides of the wall until I was able to slip my finger inside the edge. An entire panel came loose, but I didn't have enough light to see inside, so I felt around until I came across a small plastic bundle tucked tight in the corner. I couldn't believe it. This had to be at least a quarter of coke. Joey must have left it there by accident.

When I turned around, Khalid was standing in the doorway with a hurt look on his face. I cradled the drugs closer to my chest to try to hide them, but I knew it was too late. I didn't bother to say a word. Instead, I brushed past him and rushed to my room, closing the door behind me. I felt bad for all of four seconds, but that thought went out the window once I got my mirror out and spread out five neat lines. I would deal with Khalid later. For now, I needed to be on cloud nine.

Journey Clayton

Love Less Complicated

It took days for Khalid to come back. He would not answer my calls or text messages. I didn't want to go around his house, because I didn't want Vince to see me walking by. I wondered briefly if Mr. Joey knew he had gone back home. I tried to get Toya to make some sense of the situation, but all she told me to do was fall back and let the situation work itself out. I missed him so much, and wasn't really trying to hear that. She had her own shit going on, though. I'd been seeing on the news that Bunz had a bid on his head, and come to find out he'd been hiding out in Toya's spot for the past few weeks. He had a healthy bid, too, and if Toya weren't my girl, I'd turn his ass in for that change. You know how we do in the hood, though. Snitches get stitches, and she's always been in my corner, so I would never turn on her like that.

I'd been hearing rumors around the way that Gina and Khalid had something going on. I tried to ignore it, because we promised to save ourselves for each other, and I would hate to find out that I was fighting my uncle off me all this time in vain. I knew he was going through it, though. I didn't know Ms. Shanyce was turned out like that. I hooked her up when she came by, but I didn't think anything of it. She wasn't at the stage I guess that my mom was at; that's why I never paid it much attention. Now look at us.

I thought I heard the living room door open, but I wasn't sure, and I was almost certain I locked it. I hadn't seen Vince in a while, and I had some product cooked and bagged in the stash, so maybe he was coming to get it. I made sure I was cool, dressed in a pair of cotton shorts and a wife beater, with no bra or panties. I thought to get up right quick and put some on, but I didn't want him to catch me half naked and give him a reason to touch me yet again.

"Journey, where the stuff at?" Vince said, poking his head into the room. He looked zoned out as usual, probably still messing with those pancakes and syrup. I was hoping he would just get his shit and go, because I was not in the mood for him today. My mind was on Khalid and when he would speak to me again.

"In the safe," I responded in an agitated voice. I mean, where the hell else would it be? That had been the set-up since day one, so why would it change now?

He stood in the doorway longer than what felt comfortable for me. I knew he was sizing me up, and I was mad as hell that I didn't just get under the covers and pretend like I was asleep. Vince hadn't been by since me and Khalid went to the movies that night, and I knew what time it was instantly.

"What you watching, baby girl?" Vince asked as he came into my room uninvited and stood next to my bed, looking at the television like he was really interested in what was on. I took the pillow from behind my head and placed it in front of me, so that he couldn't see my bare breasts through my shirt. My heart was racing a mile a minute, and I hoped I wouldn't have to act a fool in here.

"*A Different World,*" I responded, once again hoping he would just leave. He had this simple-ass look on his face that he normally got every time he knew he was about to do something wrong. Today it wouldn't be that easy. "This is my shit. Move over so I can sit down."

"Why can't you watch it in the living room?" I asked him, placing my feet on the edge of the bed so that he couldn't sit down.

"Because I want to watch it in here with you," he responded, practically sitting on my legs.

I wanted to get up, but I didn't want him to see my ass jiggle around in these little-ass shorts. I had something for his ass today, though. Just in case he tried some stupid shit, I had gone out and got myself some protection. I was tired of living in fear, and if he was smart, he'd just leave.

He scooted back on the bed, rubbing his dry, cracked hands up and down my exposed legs. I was lying in a fetal position, so when he rubbed his hands up my legs, he went under my shorts in the back, finding that I didn't have any panties on to cover myself up. I wanted to kick myself, because I should have put the bolt lock on the door so that he couldn't get in. Khalid had me slipping. I wanted him here so bad.

"How was your birthday, Journey? What are you, fourteen or fifteen now?" he asked sarcastically, never taking his eyes from the television. "I'm fourteen."

"Good, that means I didn't miss out." I remained silent. He promised me when I was nine that once I turned fourteen, he would take my virginity. How stupid was he going to look when he found out I was not a virgin anymore? I made sure the only person in the world who ever loved me, outside of my mother, got the most important gift I could give him. Fuck Vince.

We were both silent, watching television like we'd never seen this episode before. I was trying to act like I wasn't concerned with his presence here, but on the flip side, my head was hurting and my chest was tight just thinking about what he might try to do to me.

He hooked his fingers into the waist of my shorts and tried to pull them down. I used all of my strength to keep them up. I wasn't letting him just take me like I did in the past. If he got it today, it would be well deserved, because I was fighting for my life. After being with Khalid and experiencing firsthand what love was about, I couldn't let him do this to me anymore. Khalid showed me I was worth more, and I had to prove to Vince that I was no longer scared. I couldn't keep letting this happen.

It was like everything slowed down and moved in slow motion. He kneeled down on the edge of the bed and used both hands to pull my shorts down. In my head, I began to scream, but it didn't reach my mouth, because all I heard were my uncle's muffled words and the television playing. I began to kick my legs and tug on my shorts, trying to keep him from exposing me. I just had to get behind the door and I would be able to get out of the house.

"Why are you making this harder for your-self?" he asked me as we wrestled on the bed. The heel of my foot grazed across the front of his sweat pants, and it felt like this fool was rock fucking hard. I moved back to kick him in his privates, but he grabbed my ankle and twisted it hard as hell. I didn't give a damn if he broke it in half; if I had to crawl out of here today, I would be free of this forever.

"Vince, just chill. Let me freshen up and I got you," I said to him, desperately trying to find any way I could to get up from the bed.

"Listen here, you little bitch," he said as he lay down on top of me, pinning me to the bed. "I'm taking this pussy. I've been paying for it for too long. Dead or alive, I'm taking this shit tonight."

He got up off of me and began to undress, placing a gun on the floor by the bed. Was I really ready to die tonight? I decided I was, and I knew I had to put a plan in action. Vince lay down on the bed and turned off the television. He liked silence so that he could hear himself talk shit.

I pretended like I was getting myself prepared for him as I inched closer to the door. I had my shirt up, exposing my naked breasts to him, causing him to moan out loud as he stroked his massive length from the head to the base in one fluid motion. I came out of my shirt and bent over like I was going to take off my shorts, but instead grabbing the lamp I'd picked out at Kmart at the beginning of the summer.

He never knew what hit him. I came up and brought my shoulders around, bashing him in his chest first before he could react. I kept swinging, connecting with flesh until it became soft and mushy. I made a few shots to the head as well, hoping I bashed his damn brains in. When I finally stopped, Vince was lying in a heap of crushed bones and blood.

I scooted closer and picked up the gun, not sure how to work it. He didn't look like he would be moving anytime soon, so I took that opportunity to get the hell out of dodge. Khalid would know what to do. I knew he was mad at me, but right now I needed him.

Bunz B

Last Shot

I had to make a run for it. Everyone was on lockdown except for me, and that meant someone was bound to start snitching on my ass to get less time. Toya was acting a little funny lately, too, like she might be trying to turn me in or something. I just hoped I wouldn't have to body this broad before I rolled out.

The Ville was talking, and come to find out the law has been doing random busts, going up into apartments where they thought I might be. I could see why she was getting nervous. I stashed a few thousand dollars in a floorboard in her room. Just in case I had to jet, I'd at least have something to come back to. I spoke with Vince and Choice from Toya's phone, and they agreed to make an exchange for the coke I had.

I'd been trying to get with Vince all night, but he wasn't answering his phone. He told me to meet him and Choice at the bottom of the hill, so I figured I'd just go down there and wait. I was sure he'd show up. He was a greedy nigga, so if money was involved, he was trying to get it.

Toya was lying next to me asleep. I slipped a few crushed Tylenol PM's in her iced tea while she was in the shower, so she would be out for a while. Hopefully the four pills wouldn't kill her and she'd be there when I got back.

I didn't normally go out without my crew, but they were all on lockdown, so I had no choice. I felt like I was making a mistake, like I should just stay in hiding, but I had to get this change if I wanted to be sitting pretty in Miami in the next couple of days.

I pulled up to the mouth of Bartram's Garden at three in the morning. It was darker than normal. I couldn't even see my hand in front of my face. I did as I was told, parking my car by the jungle gym and taking a seat on the sliding board. It was too quiet. I felt like something was going to happen, but I couldn't put my finger on it.

It sounded like I heard cars approaching the park, but I thought nothing of it because Choice and Vince were supposed to be meeting me here over a half hour ago. The hair on the back of my neck started standing up. Something wasn't right. Deciding to take the loss and just go back to the crib, I was suddenly blinded by flashing lights. There must have been a thousand cop cars coming from all directions, and I had nowhere to run. I didn't even have time to stash my coke.

While I was being put into one of the squad cars, I heard an officer say that they discovered Toya's body in the apartment, barely conscious. She was being rushed to the hospital as we spoke to get her stomach pumped. Shit, I almost killed the girl. There was really nothing I could do. I wouldn't be taking this stretch by myself, though. I had a whole list of names that would help me get less time. No one liked me anyway, so snitching these niggas out would be nothing.

I wondered briefly who had called the cops, because Vince and Choice never showed up, and they would have definitely gotten the work from me before calling the law. Maybe they were on their way over to me and were deterred when they saw the cops outside. I'd find out once I was in lockdown, though, because word spreads fast around the jail, so it would eventually be said what happened.

It was almost like I was in a funeral procession as the fifty or so cop cars left from down the park. I took in everything I could as we drove by, because I didn't know when would be the next time I saw daylight. It could have turned out so much better than this had I just done things differently. Fuck it now, though. I had to take this shit as it came.

Khalid Street

A Moment of Desperation

My mom was a fiend. I was just going to my room to get a few more outfits so that I could go back to Journey's when I saw her rummaging through my closet. I knew what she was looking for. My dad kept his stash in there. I thought for sure he would have cleaned everything out, but apparently she found something in the corner.

She looked confused and desperate when she saw me standing in the doorway. What could I say? She was busted, but I wasn't standing around to watch her kill herself. She rushed past me and ran into her bedroom. I was going to follow behind her, but what difference would it make? She was already out there. I'd seen it too many times.

I didn't know where my dad was at. He wasn't answering his phone.

On my way to Journey's house, I saw a ton of police cars coming from the park, and wondered briefly who they caught. I hoped it wasn't my dad as I made my way around the corner. Those same knucklehead-ass dudes were out there as I walked by.

"That was your mom, yo? She's one of my favorite customers," the one guy said, drawing a round of laughter from the group. Today would be the day he would get his ass whipped, because I was not in the mood.

"Don't sell her shit," I said through gritted teeth. I was ready to be all over these dudes, despite the odds.

"And if I do, what?" he asked, stepping to me like he was ready to throw down. I was contemplating throwing a punch when out of the corner of my eye, I saw Journey running toward me. She was running so fast that she ran right by and I had to call her name and run behind her to get her to stop. She looked frantic, and I could see that she was crying. Who was she running from? "Journey, hold up. What's wrong?"

"It's Vince. I think he's dead. He tried to rape me," she said through tears and shortness of breath.

What did she mean, he was dead? How was he trying to rape her?

"Baby, slow down. Tell me what happened." Before she could answer, I felt those guys running up behind us, but I didn't have time to react. I would just have to go out swinging and hope that Journey got away. The look on her face told me things weren't looking good, and when I turned around, I caught two bullets to the chest. I didn't drop right away, because I couldn't believe these niggas shot me. I wasn't sure if they got Journey, too, because I couldn't hear anymore and everything started to get dark. I should have kept my dad's gun on me, and then maybe I would have had a chance. All I could do was pray that help came in time and Journey was okay. Shit, I couldn't feel my legs at this moment. I was expecting a wild summer, but who knew it would turn out to end like this?

Journey Clayton

End of the Road

Who would've known that it would end like this? One day you're on top of the world, and by the end of that very same day, you're being buried in it. After all the hardships, I had hoped that one day my life would get better, but it never did. I hated the streets, I hated Vince, and I hated this neighborhood. I hated my life. We learned in school that your life is already written for you by God even before you get here, and I couldn't help but wonder why God wrote this life for me. I didn't believe in reincarnation, but if I did, I must have been a horrible person in previous lives. I was so confused about so many things, and I had no one to help me figure it out.

I should've taken another way, but how could I know that someone would try to kill me this evening? All this time I thought Vince was my worst nightmare, but I ran smack dab into a bullet. As I thought about it, though, dying may turn out to be a better option. At least I wouldn't have to deal with this cruel world anymore, and I would see my mom again. God took her away way too soon. I needed her; I always did.

It was cold as heck out here, and I didn't know if it was from the winter weather or the blood leaving my body. I tried to scoot closer to Khalid, but I couldn't feel my legs. I couldn't move my body, but surprisingly, I wasn't all that scared. The one thing Vince taught me was to live without fear. The things you can't change, you can't stress. This was one of those times where I had no choice but to let this situation play out.

Life lessons. They say everyone that you meet, you were supposed to meet for one reason or another. I knew that was why God put Khalid in my life. He helped make it more bearable to deal with my troubles. Since my birth, I couldn't remember any happy times ever.

In reality, I guess we all have to go some time, right? I just wasn't ready to go yet. When I tried to pick my head up from the hard concrete, it felt heavy, like a bowling ball. Why didn't I just keep running?

I could hear the police sirens in the distance. I wanted to yell out to Khalid that help was coming, but I couldn't move my lips. Through heavy eyelids, I saw my man lying on the ground next to me in a puddle of dark red blood, and I couldn't move. I wanted to put my head on his chest and listen to his heart beat, like I'd done so many times over the years, but I couldn't move, and it was getting colder by the minute.

Vince used to tell me to beware of haters trying to take my shine, but it started with him taking my innocence, so who could I trust? Why now, God? Didn't they teach us back in elementary school that God forgave all sins? I closed my eyes and began to pray for forgiveness. I forgave my uncle for what he did to me, even though I had already sent him to meet his maker, and I forgave the block for all the things it had done to me. Now I prayed that God would forgive me for all the lives I took by helping my uncle cook and package that deadly drug, Snow White, and I prayed . . . I prayed to make it another day.

Just as I was resting my head back on the concrete, I could hear the paramedics coming closer. Only thing is, I wasn't sure if they were going to get to me before this white light did. I could feel them trying to straighten out my crumpled body, but was I ready? All I wanted to know was if Khalid was okay. If they told me that, I could take it from there. My mom always told me to pray when I was scared; I just wasn't sure if my prayer made it to God's ears on time.